The Stone Rainbow

the
stone
rainbow

LIANE SHAW

Second Story Press

Library and Archives Canada Cataloguing in Publication

Title: The stone rainbow / Liane Shaw.
Names: Shaw, Liane, 1959- author.
Identifiers: Canadiana (print) 2019007812X | Canadiana (ebook)
  20190078138 | ISBN 9781772601084 (softcover) |
  ISBN 9781772601091 (EPUB)
Classification: LCC PS8637.H3838 S76 2019 | DDC jC813/.6—dc23

Edited by Kathryn White
Cover photo © iStock.com/Carther
Design by Melissa Kaita

Printed and bound in Canada

*Second Story Press gratefully acknowledges the support of the
Ontario Arts Council and the Canada Council for the Arts for our
publishing program. We acknowledge the financial support of the
Government of Canada through the Canada Book Fund.*

ONTARIO ARTS COUNCIL
CONSEIL DES ARTS DE L'ONTARIO
an Ontario government agency
un organisme du gouvernement de l'Ontario

Canada Council   Conseil des Arts
for the Arts   du Canada

Funded by the Government of Canada
Financé par le gouvernement du Canada |

Published by
SECOND STORY PRESS
20 Maud Street, Suite 401
Toronto, ON M5V 2M5
www.secondstorypress.ca

MIX
Paper from
responsible sources
FSC® C004071

To darling Skyler Hin Zai,
My fierce, funny, and fantastically unique grandson,
My dream for you, sweet boy, is that you will always feel
safe being exactly who you are and that you will have the
chance to grow up in a world where kindness rules and
every color has an equal place within the rainbow.
Love you forever,
Your "Emma"

If everyone just decides to treat everyone else with kindness, it all goes away. Intolerance, disrespect, racism, homophobia, misogyny, bullying, and all the other horrible words we've had to invent just to find a way to label the endless crap people seem to feel the need to throw at each other…all wiped out by one simple command. Be kind.

It's just so simple that I can't understand why everything is always so complicated.

one

"Ready yet?"

I look down at the water, a lovely shade of chlorinated blue that smells like my mother just attacked the bathroom with bleach again. It makes my eyes water, and I can barely see the pool floor that I can never quite reach no matter how hard I try to force myself down there. Swimming isn't my best trick, and it's hard to get excited about these early morning lessons when my swim coach is Cody, the world's least patient person, who thinks that everyone was born with gills just because he was.

"Yeah, it's just a little cold. Got to get used to it," I lie as I point one toe over the edge, brushing the water with the very tip. I notice that my foot is in perfect position, as if I'm about to glide across a grand stage and impress the masses with my amazing strength and dance skills. I disappear into the zone, immersed in imagining the applause of the crowd as I finish my final *grand jeté*, when suddenly I feel a hand on my back, giving me a hard shove.

"Cody!" Ryan's voice barely reaches me through the water that immerses me instead, drowning out the audience as it fills up my ears and starts pushing me down. My arms and legs instantly start flailing, which makes me swirl around in a circle like an out-of-control underwater twister. I can't remember how to get back up! My lungs feel like they're expanding to an uncontainable size, and my chest is starting to hurt as the pressure rises to an unbearable level.

I feel as if I'm on the verge of actually exploding into a million tiny pieces, never to be seen again, when a hand grabs my arm and pulls me up coughing and sputtering.

"I see we still have work to do." Cody grins as I try to re-member how to start breathing again. He takes the arm he grabbed to stop me from sinking and puts it on the edge of the pool so that I can support myself and then pushes himself back out of reach, where he stays suspended while treading water. He looks over at me cheerfully. "Oh, by the way, Jack, did I ever mention that the reason they use so much chlorine in this pool is because I scare the piss out of all my students? Like, literally."

I wipe my hand across my mouth, glaring at him while he keeps on grinning like an overfed hyena at the zoo. The chlorine tastes like it smells, which is disgusting enough, but now I could swear that I can detect traces of scared-kid pee in there as well. I think I'm going to puke. I wish Cody was closer to me so I could work on my projection.

"Cody, you are a complete ass, and you seriously suck at

teaching swimming." Ryan's butt slides over to me from where he's been sitting and watching. He reaches down, helping me pull myself out and into a sitting position.

"Is that true? About the kids?" I ask, my stomach still churning as it thinks about sending my lunch in Cody's general direction.

"That they pee in the pool? Yeah, probably. But don't worry, he had a small class today and the chlorine kills most of it anyway."

"Thanks. I feel *so* much better now," I tell him sarcastically, spitting whatever is in my mouth back into the pool...so I can swallow it later when Coach Cody tries to drown me again.

"Hey, Ryan! You're full of it. I am a perfect swimming teacher. Look at how good *you* are!" Cody yells out a delayed comeback, sounding very offended. Ryan just shakes his head.

"*You* are completely full of it. You did *not* teach me how to swim. I was swimming long before I met you."

"Yeah, well, who coached you back into shape after Jack wrecked your shoulder?"

"Jack did not wreck my shoulder, and, yes, you helped me, but your tough-guy tactics work better on someone who already knows how to swim. Jack's just learning."

I watch the two of them arguing back and forth. I'm never sure if they're actually mad or not when they do this because it's pretty much the only way they talk to each other. They met in grade five when Cody was assigned to be Ryan's "helper" and ended up turning into his friend instead. I think Ryan likes how wild and crazy Cody acts even though it obviously drives *him* crazy a lot of the time. They had a huge fight in the summer, mostly because of me, and even though they're hanging out again, I'm not sure what kind of friends they are now.

Then again, I'm not sure what kind of friends Ryan and I are either. I did wreck his shoulder when he threw himself off the bridge last spring and pulled me out of the water. After that, we ended up spending time together and it morphed into something that *seems* like friendship. But I often wonder if Ryan actually sees me as a friend or just has some kind of superhero code that says he's responsible for me forever since he saved my life. I've never talked to him about it though because I'm not sure I want to know. If I don't know the truth, I can pretend Ryan actually likes me for who I am.

I don't wonder about Cody. Ever. I don't even think about him unless we're having these swimming lessons that usually end up making me feel like I'm drowning again. Cody made it pretty clear that he's helping me because of Ryan, not because of me. That's fine. He's mostly an asshole anyway. I've never understood what Ryan sees in him. What did he call him one time? Oh yeah, misogynistic, homophobic, and relatively racist. Ryan calls that the triple threat of Thompson Mills.

I'm sure there are lots of nice people living in our small town, but unfortunately for me, Cody isn't the only triple threat. Far from it.

I'd rather have Ryan as a swim coach, but he says he can't show me regular diving techniques or how to kick properly because he has his own special swim style, compliments of his cerebral palsy. I don't know though. It still might be better than having Cody, who may be the strongest swimmer in our school but he's also working on his *Least Sensitive Person in Thompson Mills* badge. He's got a lot of competition around here, but my money is still on him.

Although I truly hate to admit it, I've learned more in the few months that he's been making me drink bleach-flavored water than I did in the years of lessons I hated having as a kid.

Bleach-and-*urine*-flavored water. I seriously feel like I'm going to throw up.

"Want to do a couple of laps while your coach figures out what torture he's going to inflict on you next?" Ryan asks. I didn't even realize they'd stopped arguing. I look at the pool where Cody is now swimming lengths, his ridiculously muscled arms flashing in and out of the water at a speed that I'll never match, even in my dreams. Ryan can, but he's always nice enough to keep it slow and steady when he's with me.

"Sure. Maybe he'll be so impressed that he'll decide we're finished for today."

"Fat chance!" Ryan laughs as he rolls into the water. Every time I watch him do it, I'm amazed all over again, something I never would say to him because he hates it when people say things like that. But it's true. I find it truly amazing that someone who can't even walk can move through the water like a dolphin that's late for school. Ryan's CP mostly affects his lower legs, and if I watch closely, I can see that they move differently from anyone else's I've ever seen swim. His thighs pump like high-powered pistons, doing all the work as if the rest of his legs were just extra attachments. It makes me feel like a wimp when I keep complaining about how hard it is to learn to swim. Not that it shuts me up.

I roll in after him, copying his actions but not nearly as smoothly. I manage to breathe first this time and get my body straightened out and moving within seconds. I surface and take a breath as Ryan turns his head and grins at me. He always looks totally happy when he's in the water. It's his safe place.

He matches my speed as we head down to the end of the pool. Once I get into the rhythm, it starts to feel good. It's as if I'm getting stronger with each stroke, slicing my arms through the water, effortlessly pushing it down and away so that I can propel myself forward. I imagine that I'm Ryan or Cody in a swim meet, pushing my strength to the limit so that I can bring my school to glory, the cheers of the crowd barely reaching my waterlogged ears as I stretch toward the finish line.

"Ow! Crap!"

I forgot that the finish line in a swimming pool is the cement wall. I put both hands on the edge of the pool, closing my eyes and wincing against the pain of smashing my head. Again.

"Are you okay?" Ryan asks, obviously trying not to laugh at me.

"Yeah, just peachy."

Cody is sitting on the edge of the pool watching me. He doesn't try *not* to laugh.

"We have to work on your dismount," he says, laughing even harder at his own stupid joke.

"Cody, leave him alone," Ryan says in that really irritating way he has of over-defending me all of the time. Maybe I *should* ask him about his superhero code.

"Oh, stop being such a mommy. The kid can talk for himself."

"Cody, go to hell." I squeeze the words out through clenched teeth. My head seriously hurts. I must have been going pretty fast.

"Later. First, I want to say that even though you tried to bash your own brains out, that was the fastest lap you've done yet. So, *you* should be thanking me, and *Ryan* should be apologizing for telling me that I'm a bad teacher when obviously I'm a pro."

I'm pretty sure there was a compliment buried in there somewhere, and I can feel my own version of Ryan's swim grin creeping onto my face.

"Thanks, Cody. You are a swimming teacher god." He looks at me happily, obviously missing the sarcasm. As usual.

"Tell me something I don't know. Ryan, do you have something to say?"

"Yeah, go get me my chair. I think we're done for today."

Cody just laughs again but does what Ryan asks bringing the chair over and locking the wheels. Ryan pulls himself out of the pool and then Cody helps him into his chair quickly and without comment. I've seen Ryan do it on his own, but when Cody is around, Ryan just automatically lets him help. Cody acts like the most self-centered jerk in the history of the known world most of the time, but he always seems to know exactly what Ryan needs and how to do it. The only thing I know how to do is push his wheelchair once in a while when the ground is rough or there's a step that's too steep for him to get over. I'd do more if he'd let me, but he doesn't seem to want my help.

We go into the locker room, where I grab my clothes and head into a cubicle to change. I know Cody is likely laughing at me for being shy, but I don't really like changing in front of other guys, especially not guys who look like him. I'm like some kind of mini-person compared to him. My head barely clears his shoulder. His arms are like tree trunks. Mine aren't even the branches. They're the pathetic little twigs that hang off the branches. I could swim a hundred laps every day for the next year and still not get muscles like his.

I throw my clothes on quickly and come out to the sinks and mirrors, grimacing as I see myself standing there. My reflection and I are not on very good terms at the moment. Nothing it shows me has much to do with who I am or how I feel inside where the rest of the world can't see me. A plain T-shirt in a really ugly shade of green that looks like something else Cody's students might leave floating in the pool. Ancient jeans that bag at my butt and end too close to my ankle because my mom bought them at Value Village.

Caterpillar camouflage so I can hide in plain sight and no one will suspect there's a technicolor butterfly hiding under the snot green and faded blue.

It's not just my clothes. My hair is black and so curly that it's always a total mess even though I bought a special conditioner to try to smooth it down. I've always wanted straight, sleek, shampoo-commercial hair. Anything would be better than this Brillo Pad sitting on my head looking like it's already been used to scrape the crap off a dozen pots and pans.

My eyes are so dark brown, it's hard to tell that I actually have pupils. My mother says they're mysterious, but Ryan calls them frightening black holes. I get them from my mother's Guatemalan parents. My eyelashes are barely there, so pale on the tips that they disappear from view. That's from my dad who is blond with green eyes.

I wonder if my hair would be better if it were blond, not that I'd have the guts to change it. Lucas dyes his hair platinum sometimes. He's the big brother of Ryan's long-distance girl-friend, Clare, and I think he's pretty close to perfect. He is so sure of himself and seems to know exactly who he is. He wears what he wants, when he wants, and doesn't seem to worry about what anyone else thinks. We met last year when Ryan, Cody, and I went on an awkward road trip to Comic Con in a city a few hours away. Lucas and his friends were so different from anyone I knew around here that it was like going to a foreign country…maybe even a foreign planet. They seemed to totally accept me, and I felt more comfortable sitting at the table with a bunch of strangers than I can ever remember feeling in the cafeteria at school.

Lucas and his friend Caleb both talk to me online some-times even though they're several years older than me. It's nice to talk to someone from outside of Thompson Mills.

It's also nice to talk to someone who's gay.

Like me.

Well, not exactly like me. They're all the way out, and I'm still most of the way in. Lucas and Caleb were the first gay people I'd ever met in my life, and it means a lot to me that they seem to actually like me and want to keep in touch.

Cody and Ryan know I'm gay. My mom and Ryan's mom. My counselor, Matthew. And maybe Officer Peabody, seeing as she's the cop who questioned me last year and might have some powers of deduction. That's it for this teeny tiny town that seems overly populated with triple threats and where the only gay person I've ever met is me.

Lots of other people *think* they know. I can't decide what's worse. Having rumors spread about me that are a mixed-up mess of true and false, or having this one truth spread about me and having people decide that everything else they've heard about me is also true.

I've heard that I'm a drug dealer. That I'm a pervert. A stalker. An alcoholic. And my personal favorite, an escaped mental patient who for some reason lives with his mother where everyone can see him.

Oh, and there's also the one about me trying to drown myself in the river, which ended up creating the great superhero of Thompson Mills.

two

"Guess what?" Ryan says to me as we move down the crowded sidewalk in front of the school.

"What?" I ask, watching as he navigates his chair expertly, weaving around people who either walk too slowly or decide to stop in front of him.

"St. Clair is gone."

"What do you mean gone?" Mr. St. Clair is the vice principal at our school. He's worked hard to create his reputation as a real tough guy with daily doses of yelling and punishing. He's never yelled at me, but I've heard him let loose on Cody a few times. Quite a few times.

"As in, he won't be here anymore. He decided to take early retirement over the holidays, and he just isn't coming back. My mom told me. I guess she heard it from someone at her school." Ryan grabs his wheels, braking hard as the girl in front of us does an abrupt about-face and almost lands in his lap. She looks down at him for a second in surprise and then smiles a little as she walks around his chair and heads off in the opposite direction. I guess she's heading somewhere more interesting than school.

"That seems kind of fast. We were only off for two weeks. I wonder what happened?" It's too bad. I've always kind of enjoyed listening to him come up with new ways to punish Cody.

"Probably got sick of Cody." Ryan laughs.

"Yeah, well he'd have to get in line."

"And you'd be at the head of it, leading the way. I know he's being a jerk in the pool, but you are really getting good."

"Not sure if that's because of him or *in spite* of him."

"Maybe you're just learning how to swim in self-defense."

"That's exactly right. If you weren't there at every lesson, I might be dead by now." I start to laugh but then stop the second I see the quick flash in his eyes. It's his *Oh my god, Jack said something about dying* look. I hate that look. It makes me feel like the victim in his drama. I know he doesn't do it on purpose, and he always puts it away quickly, but that almost makes it worse because it means it's real, something he feels inside that he's still trying to hide from me.

"Anyway, Mom said they already hired his replacement and that she's starting today." The flash is gone and the conversation is back to safer topics.

"Who is she?"

"Some woman from some city a few hours from here."

Ryan swerves a little as he wheels around a couple of guys who are walking so slowly they're almost going backward.

"Oh, well, that's nice and specific," I say, picking up my own pace a little so I can keep up with him.

"I can't remember exactly what Mom said. I do remember she thinks the new VP has a kid in our grade who will be coming to our school."

"I wonder what someone from a city school will think of TMHS." I don't have much experience with people from the city.

"I don't think anyone from the city would be too excited by life in this town. I have a few friends I met in rehab and they would probably think this place is totally boring and backward," Ryan says as he bends forward and puts his back into getting his chair up the ramp in front of the school. I always want to help him do it because it looks hard, but I offered once, and he said no so quickly that now I just keep quiet. Ryan is the only kid in our school in a wheelchair. He said that the school board had to actually order a ramp for him when he started because the school was built so long ago that it isn't accessible. He still has to use the staff bathroom because they never renovated the kids' stalls so that his chair would fit. Progressive, like everything else in Thompson Mills.

"This place *is* totally boring and backward. I can't wait until we figure out how to visit Bainesville again." I walk up the steps on the other side of the ramp, staying as close to Ryan as I can so we can keep talking. Bainesville is about three hours away from here. It isn't what you would call a huge city, but it's a lot bigger than this little dot on the map stuck in the middle of farm country. Big enough to have a Comic Con festival once a year, not to mention a university for me to escape to someday.

"Me too! If I don't get there in person soon, Clare will forget how much more handsome I am in real life than on the computer!"

"Gag me with a spoon!" Cody says, coming up behind us and pushing Ryan the rest of the way up the ramp without asking first.

"Sure, pop down to the cafeteria and grab one, and I'll be happy to." Ryan looks up at Cody and laughs.

"Yeah, yeah. You and what army? So, you guys are wanting to go to Bainesville again? Visit all the *girls?*" He's trying to get my reaction to his homophobic wit, so I just stare at him, keeping my face impassive.

"Cody! Please don't be a total asshole in the first five minutes of the day. Okay?" Ryan sounds pissed but is smiling a little at the same time. He can never decide if he loves Cody or wants to punch him. I don't have the same confusion. I pretty much always want to punch him.

Cody went to the same Comic Con as I did, but he apparently met completely different people from me. When he was introduced to Caleb, Lucas, and the rest of their group, he just saw a bunch of freaks—fags and cross-dressers, with a couple of pretty girls thrown in for him to have someone to hit on. I know he thinks I'm a freak, and I'm pretty sure he's afraid I'm going to hit on *him* some day…because all gay guys are obviously on the prowl for obnoxious homophobes who think they're the center of the universe. *Right.*

I seriously wish I'd never told Cody. My mouth got away from me when he managed to piss me off one night in the hotel room, and now he's one of the few people who know, even though he's the last person I meant to tell. I don't have to worry about him keeping my secret though. He's terrified of someone finding out that he actually associates with the guy everyone assumes is gay, so we do our swimming lessons when no one else is around, and he does his best to pretend he doesn't even know me the rest of the time. So, my secret will stay a rumor for now.

"Who the hell is that person sitting at St. Clair's desk?" Cody is standing in front of the VP's office and staring inside. There is a woman sitting there, working on the computer. I can't see her very well because Cody's in my way.

"That would be our new VP. Not that I can see anything from back here." Ryan's behind both of us, straining to see around our butts.

"New VP!" Cody jumps back, smashing into me and shouting so loudly that the woman glances over toward where I'm trying to catch my balance. She smiles, and Cody just spins away and goes over to the other side of the hall, where he leans dejectedly against the wall. Ryan follows him over. I follow Ryan because I don't want to be left standing there gawking.

"What the hell?" Cody seems honestly upset, which is weird on all kinds of levels. He fought with St. Clair pretty much on a daily basis. He's spent more time in detention because of that guy than anyone I know. He should be turning cartwheels instead of seeming like he's about to cry.

"Mom told me St. Clair decided to take early retirement. He told the board a couple of weeks ago but decided not to tell us for whatever weird reason. Maybe he didn't want to watch everyone cheering at the news or something." Ryan grins, but Cody is still looking like he just lost his best friend or something. I'm starting to think that he might have actually liked being the center of Mr. St. Clair's attention, even if it was mostly negative.

"What an asshole," Cody says, shaking his head slightly.

"I thought you'd be thrilled. You hate the guy." Ryan is confused.

"I do hate the guy. I am thrilled. This is my thrilled face." Cody smiles and manages to look like a demented gargoyle instead of someone who just got rid of his arch nemesis.

"Man, if I didn't know better, I'd think you were sad that St. Clair is gone," Ryan says, as he stares at Cody's face. Cody sneers down at him.

"Then you obviously don't know much. This is awesome. I have someone new to break in."

"Or maybe that's someone new to *break*. Pretty sure you're the reason St. Clair left." Cody nods a little, looking kind of proud.

"Could be true. I guess it's the New Year so why not have a new VP? I can make one of those resolutions to make sure she has a wonderful start to her brief time here. Talk to you later. I have work to do." He grins as he pushes himself off the wall and heads down the hallway. St. Clair is probably already a distant memory to him. Cody has the attention span of a mosquito.

"I guess we'd better get to class too. Meet you at lunch?" Ryan reaches down and unlocks his wheels.

"Yeah, see you then." I go down to my locker as Ryan wheels the opposite way. I have math this morning, which I hate, and art, which I love. I'm actually pretty good at drawing. Ryan and I have been working on a graphic novel together recently. That might be why I have gargoyles on the brain. I've drawn about a hundred of them over the past two weeks for Ryan's weird story about stone gargoyles that scope out bullies from the top of the school during the day, then come to life and beat them into submission at night. I wish I could draw so many that they actually fly off the page and start guarding the school.

Math class is as mind numbingly boring as I expected it to be. It's not that I find it difficult. I usually get decent marks in math, but I still have trouble getting excited about discovering the wonderful world of variables and equations.

Art class is a whole different situation. My father would say that art is a lot less useful than math. If he had his way, I'd be quitting this class, the same way he made me quit singing lessons when I was younger. But he left us last year, so he doesn't have his way anymore...about anything.

Art makes me feel the same as music always did, as if I can disappear into another world where I set the rules. When I draw, it feels like I'm singing with my hands, creating something beautiful that's mine and that no one else can take away from me.

"That's gorgeous!" I'm deep into my art zone, focused on blending the paints in my watercolor sky so that they feel like a gentle sunrise on a spring morning after a rainy night. I'm trying to create one of those faint rainbows that you see but aren't entirely sure is there, like an echo of lost color. The voice startles me, and I accidently knock over my water jar. It misses my painting but the water flies directly at me, splashing my sweater and dripping down into my lap.

"Crap!" I jump to my feet, brushing myself off.

"Oh my god, I'm sorry!" I look up. The voice belongs to a face that I've never seen before. I stare at it, wondering who it is while I try to remember how to talk.

Gorgeous is the right word. Dark chocolate-colored eyes with little flecks of gold that literally sparkle out at me as if someone drew them there with metallic paint. Long black eyelashes, so thick that Lucas would kill for them. Chestnut-brown hair that actually shines like a shampoo commercial and is long enough to be tied back into a ponytail that probably got some people talking when they saw him coming down the hall in this school full of buzz cuts. Tall—taller than Cody—with wide shoulders and arms that I imagine are pretty toned under his bright red sweater.

"What?" *Oh, good. That's a brilliant response.*

"I said I'm sorry I startled you. I'm glad the water didn't wreck your painting. I hope you're not too soaked." His voice matches his looks. It sounds like he should be narrating movies or reading the news on TV.

"Soaked? Oh, no. Just a little damp." I brush a bit at my sweater, trying to look cool and probably not succeeding. He's smiling at me, and I can feel my cheeks turning red. My stomach is jumping around as if I'm nervous, which doesn't make sense because there's nothing to be nervous about just because some guy made me spill my water.

"Well, good. I wouldn't want to make enemies on my first day. I'm Benjamin, by the way." He holds out his hand to shake. I reach mine toward him but snatch it back quickly when I realize that it's wet from my sweater. I wipe it down the side of my pant leg and then take his hand and give it a quick shake. My stomach goes into overdrive.

"Hi. I'm Jack. Jack*son.*" *Why'd I say that?* I never use my full name. Most people around here don't even know my name is Jackson. I've always sort of thought it would just add to my problems. Jack sounds shorter and less sweet.

"Nice to meet you, Jackson. Guess I should let you go and finish your work."

Say something intelligent. Or funny. Welcome him to the school. Ask him to lunch.

"Yeah, I guess." *Oh, perfect. Really warm and welcoming.*

I watch him go over to the other side of the room and sit down, trying not to punch myself in the forehead. What's wrong with me? I'm not exactly a social whiz kid, but I'm usually at least capable of basic speech.

I look back at my painting, trying to remember what I was doing with it, but there seems to be an insect colony trying to get loose in my gut and I can't concentrate. I take another look across the room and accidentally catch his eye. He grins and gives me a little wave. I can feel my cheeks flare up again, and I quickly shift my gaze to my work.

I can't believe he caught me looking. This is so embarrassing.

Then it occurs to me that if he caught *me* looking, *he* was looking too. The thought fills my stomach with hyperactive buzzing as the insect colony breaks free, flying around and around until my whole body feels like it's vibrating and I've completely forgotten what I'm supposed to be doing.

three

A whole week has disappeared, and I haven't talked to Benjamin again. I've been doing my best to watch everything he does and avoid him at the same time, which is a lot harder than it sounds. It is seriously starting to make my brain hurt, but I can't seem to make myself stop. I think about him all the time even though I don't know anything about him except his name and the fact that he's the son of the new VP, Mrs. Lee. Which means he's from the city, according to Ryan, and would never be interested in some little townie like me.

Not that he'd be interested anyway. I don't know what I'm saying, even in my own mind! I've never been attracted to anyone live and in person before. There never seemed to be any point, seeing as I'm only interested in guys, and I don't know of any guys in our town who would be caught dead or alive looking at me.

I also don't know what the deal is with Benjamin. Why am I breaking my self-imposed rule about even imagining futile relationships with real people who go to my school or live in my town? Maybe it's because he's from somewhere else and seems different from everyone around here. I don't know. He probably has a girlfriend back home who texts him every five minutes and is just waiting for him to come home once his mother-imposed exile is over.

He seems like such a nice guy. He's always talking to people, making them smile. The girls have noticed him by now, and there's always someone following him around, trying to get his attention. I follow him around too, but far enough away that I'm making sure I *don't* get his attention. He doesn't need another stalker.

"Have you met the new guy yet?" Ryan's voice interrupts my thoughts and I jump guiltily. We're at his locker, getting ready to go home, and I've been staring at Benjamin down at the other end of the hall. *Did Ryan notice?*

"Um, no. Not really. Well…kind of. I guess. He's in my art class." *Very smooth, Jack. He'll never suspect a thing.*

"He seems okay. He's in my English class. We've talked a few times. He's actually from the same city where I had my last couple of surgeries. It's like five or six hours from here by car and about twice the size of Bainesville, so he'll find this place small."

"Oh. That's interesting." *Or not.* Figures that Ryan would have more in common with him than I do.

"He wasn't super thrilled that he had to move here in

senior year, but his mom really wanted the job, so he didn't have a choice. I bet it sucks to be in a new school in your last year and be the kid of the VP though." He puts a couple of books into his bag and slams his locker shut.

I just nod and follow him to the front door, taking a quick look over my shoulder as we go. I just about pass out when my eyes instantly latch onto Benjamin's face, which is now about an arm's length behind me. Close enough to touch but a million light years away. He grins at me, and I smile back quickly before turning around and grabbing the back of Ryan's chair, pretending he needs my help.

"I'm good, Jack," Ryan says, sounding mildly pissed with me as he puts extra force into wheeling himself so that I'll let go. If I was Cody, he'd let me push him from here to the next county.

We head down the sidewalk in silence. I'm beside him, speed walking so that I can keep up. He wheels fast, especially on the way home from school because it's mostly downhill. We get to the corner in less than ten minutes.

"Do you want to come with me and see if my mom has something worth eating at the restaurant?" There are two alternating so-called chefs at the restaurant where my mom works as a waitress and knowing who's working on a particular day makes a huge difference to the number of stomach cramps you'll have after eating there.

"No, I don't think I have time today. I have a stupid English essay due next week that I haven't started. My mom made me promise to get a rough draft done today so that she can edit it with me. The joys of having a principal for a parent."

"At least she's not the principal at your school."

"Yeah, that's true. I've never been in the same school as her. It's hard enough having her riding my ass over homework at home. I think that Benjamin kid might have trouble with some guys at school if his mom starts getting on their case."

"Kids like Cody?"

"Oh, definitely Cody. He's already been to the office once since she got here. I'm sure he'll be trying to take it out on her kid. He's such a jerk sometimes."

One of these days I'm going to ask him why that jerk is the only person he ever allows to help him.

"How did you know that Clare was the one?" I ask instead, surprising both of us. Ryan isn't a big fan of talking about his feelings. Or anything else remotely personal.

"The one what?" he asks. There's no smile so I can't tell if he's kidding or not.

"The one you want to…be with, date, whatever you call it."

He squints up at me, with one hand shielding his eyes from the sun. "I'm not sure. She's beautiful and nice. Smart and funny."

"Lots of girls are all those things but don't live three hours away. There has to have been something about her that was different to make it worth the effort." He shrugs, still squinting and shielding. He closes his eyes for long enough that I can't tell if he's thinking or passed out.

"I think…it was the way she looked."

"You already said she's beautiful."

"No, I don't mean that. I mean the way she looked *at* me, not to me. It was like she actually saw me." I'm not sure what he means so I don't say anything. My face obviously says enough because he smiles and tries again.

"Most girls I meet see a guy in a chair. Sometimes they see the guy first and the chair second, and sometimes it's the other way around. But they always see both as separate things and are super aware of the fact that I can't walk. That usually ends the relationship before it starts. Clare saw a guy who happens to be in a chair, like it's a piece of me and it matters but at the same time it doesn't. It's kind of like the way Cody has always been with me. I'm just another guy to him, not some handicapped kid. Does that make any sense?"

"Yeah, actually, I think I get what you're saying." Now that he's said it, I can see what he means about Cody. He treats Ryan like anyone else, bugging him and giving him a hard time and then casually helping him like it's no big deal.

"Why are you asking?"

"I don't know. Just been thinking about relationships recently," I answer. Ryan nods slightly.

"Well, if you need relationship advice, maybe you should call Clare. She loves talking about relationships. Mostly ours, but I'm sure she'd be more than happy to talk to you."

"You wouldn't mind?"

"Why would I mind? It's not like you're going to try to steal her away, right?"

He grins. I smile back. A gay joke. That's cool. He usually avoids the topic. He was the first person I came out to in this town, and he's mostly fine with it, so long as we don't talk about it. Out of sight, out of mind.

Or better yet, not *out* at all.

Clare might be the perfect person to talk to about Benjamin. Better than Ryan, who is definitely not ready to give me relationship advice unless I suddenly develop a passion for girls. Even then, I think he'd pass me on to Clare.

"I'll text you her contact info, but I think she already friended you on Facebook, right? Just a warning that she'll want to put you on-screen because she says it's better to interact with someone when you can look them in the eyes."

"Okay, thanks. I might give her a try."

He seems like he wants to ask something about my sudden interest in relationships, but then he just smiles.

"She'll love it. Giving advice is her absolute favorite thing. Anyway, I'd better go, or the essay police will be on my case. Maybe if I get enough done, we can hang later and work on some graphics for the novel."

"Okay, sounds good. See you later."

I was going to go to the restaurant and see if Mom would feed me, but I change my mind and head for home.

"Hey, Jack, this is so nice. I've always wondered why you never talk to me!"

Clare's face grins at me from my laptop screen. As soon as I got in the door, I checked to see if she was online, but now that she's sitting there staring at me, I don't know what to say.

"I didn't know if you would want to talk to me."

"You are my boyfriend and my brother's friend. Of course, I'm interested in you." She smiles sweetly. She is definitely beautiful.

"How is Lucas?"

"He's great. He and Jamal are heading down to Hawaii for a little trip next week. I have a feeling that Jamal might be popping the question."

"What question?"

"The *will you marry me* question. I could be wrong because they haven't been together all that long, but Jamal seems super crazy about Lucas, and he's a few years older, so I think he might be heading in that direction. I hope so. I like him, and he makes Lucas happy. Lucas would love to be the star of his own wedding. I'm pretty sure he would create the most amazing wedding dress."

A wedding. I've never even thought about getting married someday. I'm too obsessed with wondering if I'll ever go on a date.

A wedding *dress*. If a miracle happened and I ever did get married, I'd probably chicken out and end up wearing a tux in basic black. I imagine Lucas will create something beautiful in every color of the rainbow, worthy of landing on the cover of a magazine.

I know a lot of people call that cross-dressing, but I don't understand why there needs to be a label at all. I think it should just be called getting dressed.

I also know it's a myth that all "cross-dressing" men are gay, just like the belief that all gay guys want to wear feminine clothes. But some of us do…or at least we want to try it outside in the daylight instead of in the closet where it's kind of dark and hard to see how we look. I envy Lucas's unique style so much that I swear I can feel my skin turning green every time I see him. He can rock a pair of jeans just as easily as a designer dress. I wish I had his courage. I dream all the time about wearing what I want, when I want, and not having to worry about other people's opinions.

"Earth to Jack." Clare's voice pulls me out of the inside of my head, and I smile self-consciously.

"Sorry. Just imagining Lucas in a wedding dress, or whatever he might decide to come up with for his big day. He has a pretty creative style."

"That's putting it mildly. But I'm pretty sure you didn't contact me to talk about Lucas. What's up? Are you okay? Things going better with your mom?"

Her eyes look concerned, but it doesn't bother me the way it does when Ryan stares at me like that.

"That's a good question. She's making an effort to understand, I think. She doesn't talk about it much, but she isn't trying to get me to her priest for an exorcism either."

"Well, at least she loves you enough to try. Not all of Lucas's friends were that lucky when they came out."

"Yeah, he told me. But it's hard to feel lucky when I know she wishes I wasn't gay. She wants me to be straight and get married and have babies." Clare makes a face.

"*Straight*. As if everyone else is crooked or something. Anyway, I guess all you can do is give her time. Someday she'll understand that you can be gay, get married, *and* figure out a way to have babies." She looks at me expectantly. She's obviously figured out I didn't call her to talk about my mother.

I take a deep breath.

"So, there's a new guy at my school." She smiles widely but doesn't say anything. "And he's gorgeous and seems friendly and smart, and I can't stop thinking about him, and I don't know what to do about it." The words come rushing out, tripping over each other in their hurry, and probably sounding like a mess of nonsense syllables to Clare.

"That's great," she says, nodding as if I said something intelligent.

"I don't know what it is. I've barely talked to him, and besides, I don't even know if he's gay or not. I don't know why I'm feeling this way if he isn't, but how do I know?"

"I don't think anyone knows anything when they first meet someone and feel that…thing."

"Thing?"

"Like a chemical reaction or something. I felt it when I saw Ryan."

"But it's probably not a good idea to feel chemical reactions for someone who isn't gay when you are. Have you ever heard of gaydar?"

"Yeah, Lucas says he has it." She laughs.

"Do you think it's real? That you can somehow sense if someone else is gay?"

"I don't know. Maybe you just sense that the person is interested. If a guy is interested in another guy, chances are he's gay. I don't know if that's gaydar or just love."

"Love? I think I'm a long way from that."

"Hey, you never know. It has to start somewhere."

"How do I find out if he's gay or not? I can't just walk up to him and ask. And I don't want to keep feeling this way about him if he isn't."

"No one ever knows if there's a chance or not at the very beginning. Just talk to him. Find out more about him. If he is your guy, it'll happen."

My guy. The thought gives me a little shiver.

"But I don't want to keep feeling all…stalker-guy if there's no chance."

She laughs again. "Don't stalk him then. Try being his friend instead."

"Can I be his friend with all of these feelings messing up my head?"

"You can try. Welcome to the wonderful world of falling in love, Jack."

Falling in love. I never thought I'd do that with anyone, let alone someone right here in Thompson Mills.

My dad has this expression: There isn't a snowball's chance in hell.

My mom would probably think I'd end up down there with the snowball if I actually fell in love with a guy.

A gorgeous guy with big brown-and-gold eyes who smiles at me in a way that no one has ever smiled at me before.

Except he might stop smiling once he gets to know more people and starts hearing all the rumors about me.

Or worse, finds out the truth.

four

The story has become a town legend, fact and fiction blended together into some kind of conversational smoothie that people still talk about even though it feels like it happened a lifetime ago.

Less than a year now, but it feels like forever to me.

Ryan the hero, flinging himself out of his wheelchair to save the poor little gay kid from drowning.

At first everyone called it an accident. It even made it into the local news because nothing much ever happens in a town as small as ours, and the idea of someone who can't walk managing to save someone who can't swim was pretty fascinating to the outside world for about fifteen minutes.

In my world, it moved from an accident to a suicide attempt pretty quickly, and everyone started to look at me like I had morphed into a bigger freak than they'd thought I was in the first place. And that made everything seem so much worse.

They made me start counseling before I even left the hospital. My counselor, Matthew, keeps trying to make me talk about it. He thinks it's important for me to understand what I was doing at the water that day so that I can find a better way of dealing with my problems than trying to float away from them.

He wants me to say that I was trying to kill myself.

That I wanted to die.

But the thing is, I don't know if that's true.

* * *

I can still close my eyes and see the yellow fabric floating out from my hands, soft and shimmery, like an extension of the sunlight just waiting for someone to slip it on and blend into the morning.

I hesitated for a few seconds, trying to shake off the realization that this was a seriously bad idea. What if someone saw me? Everything—absolutely everything—would end if someone saw me.

I looked over at the bridge and the street beyond it. Still deserted. I put the skirt over my head and tugged it down over my jean jacket until it sat over the waistband of my pants. It looked lumpy with my jeans underneath, but there was no way I could risk taking the time to get them off.

I closed my eyes, lifted the edges of the skirt, and began to twirl until I couldn't feel anything but the wind moving me around and around, endless circles with no beginning and no end. I wanted to do it forever, just keep dancing until I could forget everything.

But I couldn't dance fast enough to erase the words written across my mind. The reminders that I'd been living in a town where no one, not even my own mom, wanted me to be myself.

My mom. The thought of her made my heart hurt, as if someone had reached down into my chest and started to squeeze. I wanted to tell her who I was so badly, but I was so scared of what she'd do that I felt like I was going to faint every time I imagined the conversation.

What was I thinking—dancing around where someone might see me and laugh?

Or worse.

My feet just stopped. I stood there, staring at the river. The water glistened in the sunlight. Soft. Calm.

I moved forward to the edge and started to walk slowly in. My skirt tripped me a little as it soaked up the liquid, and I had to hold it up a bit, so I didn't fall. I couldn't really swim. I always hated lessons, and my mom finally took pity on me before I actually figured out how to stay on top of the water.

Mom. I moved forward, trying to put her out of my mind. Trying to put everything far away from where I had to think. The water felt wonderful. Each step deeper made me feel like everything was just leeching out of me and floating away. The fist around my heart loosened, and I wondered why I'd ever hated swimming lessons in the first place. My whole body felt loose, almost the way dancing makes it feel, but different. Better.

I kept walking until the gentle coolness was up to my chest and then my chin. I could hear nothing but my own heart beating, thump-thumping against my ribs until it almost hurt but felt good at the same time.

The water floated up around my cheeks, teasing me a little. What would happen if I took just one more step? Would I float? Drift away from everything and everyone until nothing hurt anymore?

So tired of it hurting.

I took one more step and then, suddenly, the water grabbed hold of me, pulling me under and wrapping around me like a huge, heavy, wet blanket that pushed me down until I couldn't breathe. My heart started to pound at an uncontrollable pace, and I felt like it was going to shoot right out of my chest as all of the light disappeared, and I couldn't even tell if my eyes were open or shut.

I didn't know until later that Ryan was sitting up on the bridge, calling out to me, trying to get me to stop moving.

❋ ❋ ❋

So much has changed since that day. When I replay it in my mind, it's almost as if I'm watching a movie about someone else's life, and I'm trying to figure out the character's motivations from my seat in the audience instead of wandering around inside my own head. And I don't want to watch it anymore. I just want to put it away so that I can pretend it never happened.

After everything that happened last summer, I decided that

I'm going to move to Bainesville after graduation. I applied to school there, but even if I don't get in, I'm still moving there to work. I need to live somewhere that isn't here. I want a chance to try to be myself in a place where people haven't already decided what they think about me.

I don't want to be the freaky kid who had to be saved from drowning. I want to leave that part of me behind, in the back of my closet where there will be extra space because my makeup has come away with me to my new life. I had planned to keep a low profile this year so that I could graduate and get away from this place without adding anything new to my less than stellar reputation.

But then Benjamin arrived on the scene.

I don't even know him. But for some reason, I can't sit on the sidelines and watch other people narrate my life in a way that will make him want to close the book on me before he gets past the first chapter. I want him to know that there's more to my story than the opinions of other people who don't even know me.

Which probably means I'll have to try to remember how to talk the next time I see him.

five

"Hi." I get the single word out of my mouth, telling myself to stand my ground and resist the urge to run. Benjamin looks up from his painting of…I want to say a dog, but it could be a pony.

"Hey!" He gives me his awesome smile.

"How's it going?" I ask, trying to smile back with an equal level of awesomeness. My face feels strange, and I have a bad feeling that I resemble one of the gargoyle drawings I discarded because it was too weird to use in Ryan's novel. I gesture toward his artwork so he'll look away until I can get my face under control.

"How's my crap-ass painting going, or how is life in general going?" He laughs and, shaking his head, glances down at the dog/pony.

"Either one. That's an interesting…dog?" *Please let it be a dog.*

"Yeah, totally interesting, seeing as it's a deer."

Shit. Wrong on both counts. At least pony would have been closer. I can feel my cheeks betraying me, flaring up like they always do when I'm making a fool of myself.

"Oh, yeah, I see it now."

"Liar. I suck at drawing. I like the abstract stuff, where no one knows what you're trying to draw so they can't say you did a crappy job."

I think abstract painting is all about using color and lines in a way that creates an impression of different things to different people. I personally believe it's actually much harder than realism. Probably shouldn't say that out loud though. Telling him I think he's wrong is likely not the best way to start a friendship.

"Yeah, me too," I lie. *Good choice! Lying is so much friendlier.*

"You can draw like crazy though. Maybe you could give me some pointers?"

"Sure. Umm, well, one thing I find really helpful when I'm drawing is to use a photograph to start from, just to get the proportions and details right." He grins at me as he pulls a piece of paper out of his bag. It's a photo of a deer.

"I did that. And here is the wonderful result. My lopsided dog with long legs and knobby knees."

"Well, you could just slim out the body a bit, like so." I borrow his pencil and make a few lines, streamlining the torso and giving the legs some muscle tone. "And give more definition to the hooves so they look like—"

"Hooves instead of paws," Benjamin finishes for me, watching me work. He's leaning forward, so his chest is brushing against my arm as I work. My hands are starting to sweat a little, and I'm not sure I can hold on to the pencil long enough to finish.

"Just trim the ears back a little and lengthen the nose, and there you go. It's a deer." I turn my head and he's right there. We're nose to nose, and I can't stop myself from staring.

He has a really nice one, just a tiny bit crooked on one side as if maybe he broke it once upon a time, which just makes him even better-looking, kind of edgy and tough. I keep on staring at it, wondering if he got in a fight or maybe swam into a pool wall before I realize what I'm doing and jerk myself back out of his personal space. I drop the pencil on the table and wipe my sweaty hand on the back of my pants, hoping he doesn't notice.

"Thanks, that's awesome," he says, seeming oblivious to my sweat-drenched palms and inappropriate nose gawking. "I'm glad you stopped to talk. And not just because you fixed my work. You never talked to me after the first day I came here. I was kind of thinking I'd done something to piss you off."

Damn! I was hoping he hadn't noticed. Or is it good that he did notice? What's better? Noticing or not noticing?

Right now, he's probably noticing that I'm just standing here instead of answering him.

"No—nothing like that! I'm just…shy, I guess. I don't always do well with new people." *Good answer. You definitely don't sound like a loser now.*

"When I saw you that first day, I was kind of hoping you

were friend material. I don't have any of those around here just yet." He smiles that smile, and I have to lean casually against the table so I don't fall down and embarrass myself.

"I'm not exactly overloaded with them either." *Oh, wow, Jack, this just keeps getting better and better!*

"I don't know why. You seem like a pretty cool person." I smile at him, so startled by the almost compliment that I feel a little light-headed for a second. Either he hasn't heard what people say about me yet or he hasn't made the connection between the words and the face.

"There are people around here who wouldn't agree." *Way to go. Let him know you're Mr. Unpopularity. That'll impress him.*

"There are stupid people in every school. I do my best to avoid them, and if I can't avoid them, I just tune them out." He makes very deliberate and direct eye contact, and suddenly I can see it in there. That he's heard at least some of what people say about me but he's talking to me anyway.

I wonder if he's heard the one about the insane asylum yet.

"Maybe you can teach me how to do that."

"I would love to," he says, the gold flecks in his eyes jumping out at me, making my heart do a slow roll in my chest.

Calm down, Jack. Remember what Clare said. Just friends.

"My friend Ryan and I are going to the Supe after school for fries. You could come if you want, and we can show you around downtown." Three stores, a restaurant, and the post office. I hope he doesn't pass out from all the excitement.

"The *Supe?*"

"The Superior Restaurant. The food mostly sucks, but everyone hangs out there anyway, seeing as it's the only restaurant in town. My mom works there."

"Oh yeah? That's nice. You can hang with your friends and your mom at the same time." I look at his face to see if he's making fun of me, but he looks serious, like he actually thinks it's nice and not pathetic. Over his left shoulder, I suddenly notice the teacher is staring at us, looking less than pleased. She likes me because she thinks I'm artistic, but that doesn't mean she won't bitch me out and embarrass me.

"Anyway, I'm going to get in shit if I don't go back to my seat. If you want to come, just meet us at the front of the school after the final bell."

"Sounds good."

I head back to my seat, trembling a little in amazement at my own success. I can't believe this. He noticed me? Thought I'd be friend material? And I've been avoiding him so much that he thought I was pissed with him. How stupid could I be?

No. Don't do that. That doesn't matter now. Focus on the positive. What matters is that I did it. Right? I actually talked to him, and it was better than any dialogue Ryan could have written for one of his stories.

I spent the rest of the day in a fog, wandering around my classes as if I were dreaming them. I made about a million mistakes in math class and forgot to bring my books to history. After school, on the way to my locker, I walked into a wall instead of watching where I was going because I was busy wondering if Benjamin would actually come with us.

"Are you ready?" I walk quickly over to Ryan's locker when the endless school day is finally over.

"What?" He's checking his phone, reading something.

"I said are you ready to go?"

"Um, no. I haven't even opened my locker yet." He looks at me strangely and reaches up to undo his lock. He's taking his sweet time about it, and I'm trying not to jump out of my skin waiting for him. What if Benjamin decides we're not coming and just leaves?

"Oh, right. Okay. Well, maybe I'll just wait for you out front."

"Why? It's raining." He starts putting books away and taking others out. Slowly and carefully, like he's got all the time in the world. Seriously, any minute now I'm going to shed like a snake if I don't get moving.

"It's just drizzling and I…need some air. Oh, and I invited the new guy to come with us. Hope that's okay."

"Benjamin? Sure. He's cool."

"You've already met him?"

"Yeah, I told you before, he's in my English class. We've talked a few times. He's nice." I look at him in surprise. How could I have forgotten that? My brain is blowing so hot these days that it must be melting.

I need to cool it. Literally. I'm getting so far ahead of myself that I've disappeared from my own view.

"Anyway, I'll just go and wait at the front door in case he decides to come and is looking for us," I say casually, making it clear I don't care if the guy joins us or not.

I go to the door, trying not to run in the hall. It would suck if I didn't make it there in time because Benjamin's mom had to stop me and recite the school rule book. I get there at a fast walk and try to figure out the best place to stand so I can't possibly miss him. Why wasn't I more specific? The front of the school is huge and there are people everywhere. He could walk right by and think I stood him up!

Or...I could just calm the hell down. It's just fries at the Supe with Ryan, not a date for the prom.

"Jackson!"

I spin so fast at the sound of Benjamin's voice that I actually fall off the step.

"Oh, hi," I say, sounding super cool as I cling to the railing so I don't dramatically fall all the way down the cement staircase.

"I thought maybe I'd missed you guys. It's busy out here," he says cheerfully as I manage to pull myself up and into a standing position. I lean casually on the railing.

"Yeah, well it's a pretty big school."

"My last school was about three times this size, but we had staggered entry so everyone wasn't cramming the stairs at the same time." Three times this size. He must think we're so pathetically "small town." And I'm taking him to the Supe, which will just reinforce the image of this being a total backwoods.

"This place must feel small to you."

"I guess. But it's not too bad."

"Not too good either?"

"Time will tell." He smiles, and I almost fall down the step again.

"Hey, Benjamin." Ryan appears at the top of the ramp beside where we're standing.

"Hey, Ryan. Do you need any help with that?"

"Nope, I'm good. Meet you at the bottom." He wheels down the ramp fast enough that it looks like it might be fun.

We walk down the stairs, much more slowly because we're behind a bunch of kids who are stopping every two seconds to show each other things on their phones. We don't bother trying to talk until we get clear of the school and are on the sidewalk heading downtown.

"So how much does living in Thompson Mills suck?" Ryan asks. Benjamin laughs.

"Oh, it's not so terrible. I was just pissed that I had to come here in senior year. I was in my last school all the way through, so it would have been nice to graduate with my friends. I thought my dad might save me by staying behind, but he decided to take a sabbatical and come with us, so here I am."

"I imagine our grad will be pathetic compared to what your school would have done."

"I don't even know what they're doing for grad. What do you guys do here?"

"Oh, it's really exciting. There's a ceremony and then a dance in the school gym."

"Oh. Well, I think there's a little more to it back home, but that's all good. Maybe they'll have fired my mom by then and I'll be back there."

Benjamin grins. Ryan smiles back. I just keep walking while trying to ignore the cheerful way he talks about leaving. Of course he would want to go back home. He's probably the most popular guy in his school. I have to stop twisting myself up about some guy who most likely loves the ladies and has a string of them waiting for him.

"So, here's downtown," I announce as we turn onto the originally named Main Street. Benjamin glances down the street, appearing extremely underwhelmed.

"Well, you did warn me," he says.

"It just gets better. I think Charlie is working today."

"Oh, great. I always love those burnt burgers from old Char Char," Ryan says, making a face. "The Supe has two cooks. Stevie, who kind of sucks, and Charlie, who really sucks and thinks everything needs to be cooked until it's crispy. Even the oatmeal."

"Sounds great."

We get to the restaurant, and Benjamin opens the door and holds it for Ryan because our really advanced town doesn't have those automatic door openers anywhere but at the community center. We go inside and head for a booth at the back. Mom sees us right away and gives me a little wave.

"That's your mom? She's pretty," Benjamin says. I'm surprised. I've never thought of her as pretty. I've never thought of her as *not* pretty either. I just think of her as *Mom*.

I stare at her for a second. She has her pink uniform on with the white running shoes that she says are the only thing that keep her feet from dying. Her black hair is tied back with a pink ribbon to match the uniform. I watch her smile at a customer, her dark eyes crinkling a bit at the corners as she laughs a little at something he says. He's an old guy who comes here all the time. There's a bunch of them who hang out in the restaurant every day, just for something to do. They all love my mother because she's so nice to them and remembers their names and what they like to eat. Watching her now, I realize that she probably seems like a young girl to them, and they likely think she's flirting. She finishes serving the old guy and comes over to our table.

"Hi, sweetheart. Hello, Ryan. Fries and burgers?" She looks at us and then over at Benjamin. "Hello." She looks at me, eyebrows raised. *Right. Introduce the guy.*

"Hi, I'm Benjamin. New in town. These guys took pity on me and are showing me around." Benjamin beats me to it with his usual level of class and style. My mom looks impressed.

"There's not much showing to be done, I'm afraid. There's just Main Street and the bridge." She glances at me quickly as she says that last word. She doesn't really like to think about the bridge much and obviously wishes she hadn't accidentally let the word out.

"Is Charlie on today?" Ryan asks, pulling her gaze over to him and changing the subject before it can even turn into one.

"Unfortunately, yes. So, just fries might be safer. Or maybe even just soda?"

"We'll risk the fries, Mrs. Pedersen. Thanks."

We sit back to wait. Benjamin looks around the room.

"There aren't too many people like me in this town, are there?" he asks.

six

I freeze for a few seconds, wondering what he means by that. Does he mean there aren't too many guys with long hair around here? Or is he talking about people who wear clothes that aren't made out of denim or flannel? I know there aren't many guys around here with dark chocolatey eyes that sparkle like miniature stars every time they smile, but I'm guessing that is *not* what he's talking about.

I know what I *wish* he was saying…the one thing that I'm afraid to even think about because it would be really wonderful and absolutely terrifying at the same time.

"What do you mean?" Ryan asks him, which is a more practical approach than sitting here like a zombie while my brain goes into hyperdrive.

"I mean, I've only seen one other Asian person since I got

here, and that was at the gas station before you actually get to town."

Now we both stare at him. I can feel the breath I didn't even know I was holding come whooshing out as I totally deflate.

Asian?

"That's Henry. He owns the place," Ryan says.

"Henry. That's a good Chinese name. Almost as good as Benjamin." He watches us watching him for a second and then laughs. "I'm half Chinese. My dad came here from China when he was in his twenties. That's where the Lee comes from. Pretty common surname in his world. Benjamin comes from my mom's side."

I stare at him, wondering why I hadn't noticed both sides of his personal equation before when it's so obvious now that he's pointed it out. Ryan pokes me, and I finally look away.

"Sorry. I didn't mean to stare." I can feel the blush starting. Great. Now my mom will come back and see my face and ask questions when we get home.

"It's okay. I guess I do lean toward my mom's looks."

"Do you speak Chinese?" Ryan asks.

"*Dui.* That's Mandarin, which I can speak fairly well on a good day. I started going to Saturday Mandarin school when I was five. My dad and grandparents both speak Cantonese as well, but I only know a few words."

"That's still pretty impressive," Ryan says.

I'm just sitting here listening, trying to get my cheeks to settle down before my mom comes back.

"There are two main languages that most people here know about. There are a couple billion people in China though, so there are all kinds of different dialects and languages there. It's an amazing place. We went last summer, and I couldn't believe how many people there were everywhere you go. I met like a gazillion relatives."

"Here you go, boys," Mom says, putting three plates of fries in front of us and pulling a bottle of ketchup out of her pocket. We all thank her like good little boys. She smiles and goes off to charm the other customers.

We start shoving fries down our throats, eating fast so we don't notice the three-day-old grease that they were obviously fried in.

"Oh, the other thing I was wondering about is..." Benjamin pauses as he pours some more ketchup on his plate, "where are all the gay guys?"

I swallow without remembering to chew and immediately start to choke on a fry. Lucky for me, the extra grease helps it slide the rest of the way down so Super Ryan doesn't have to do the Heimlich on me.

"Pardon?" I say, gasping and coughing while Ryan just watches without bailing me out. He's smiling slightly as if he's enjoying the show.

"The gay guys. I need someone to take to grad if we're still here." Benjamin grins.

"Oh, didn't I tell you? Benjamin is gay. He told me that during English class." Ryan increases the wattage on his smile until I really want to put it out with my fork.

"No, I think I would have remembered that."

Benjamin takes a quick glance around the room again and then looks directly at me.

"So, I can't be the only one. No town is that small."

I look over at Ryan, who's still lighting up the restaurant with his grin, and then back at Benjamin, who obviously doesn't have gaydar or he would know that there is at least one rumor about me that's true. Or maybe he does know and is just playing with me. Either way, I have a decision to make here. I take a deep breath.

"It definitely feels that small sometimes. I'm the only gay guy I've ever met here. Until now, I guess." I try a smile that I'm pretty sure is as awkward as it feels.

Benjamin stares directly into my eyes as his grin morphs into his trademark smile, gold flecks sparkling until they drown out Ryan's grinning face and everything else in the room.

My heart is beating so fast that I'm sure everyone can hear it. My head is buzzing with a thousand thoughts all blended together so that I can't think at all. I see my mother coming across the room and one thought manages to make it through to the surface.

I hope to God she didn't hear Benjamin just announce that he's gay.

Ryan and Benjamin spend the rest of our time together talking about inconsequential, boring stuff like TV and sports and homework. We walk partway home together and say good-bye casually, as if nothing monumentally important just happened that could possibly change life as I know it. I walk the rest of the way home in a daze, my mind still whirling around in dozens of different directions at the same time.

● ● ●

I message Clare the minute I get into my room so that I can talk this out before my head explodes and makes a big mess on the floor.

"But what are the odds that the only other gay guy in town would happen to end up being interested in me?"

"Don't worry about that."

"But that's the biggest thing to worry about. It's like, what if you went to an all girls' school and suddenly there was a guy there? Would you fall for him just because he was the only guy?" Clare looks at me and laughs.

"I don't think that's the same scenario. He might be the only guy, but I'd have a lot of competition in a school full of girls. I might not even get a chance to look at him."

I think for a second. She's right. It's not the same thing. I wouldn't have any competition at our school. At least not that I know of. But that's the problem. It's like buying cereal that you don't particularly like just because it's the only box left on the shelf. You eat it because it's the only thing available, not because you actually want it.

"But that's the point. I wouldn't want him to pick me because I'm the only box of cereal on the shelf." Clare gives me a confused look.

"Um…sure, no one would want that. Jack, you're seriously overthinking this. Nothing changes now that you know he's gay. You still need to get to know him, see if there's anything there."

"Oh, there's something there. I can't stop thinking about him. Every time I see him at school my hands sweat and my stomach starts jumping around."

"That's sweet. It's called chemistry."

"I don't even know if *he* feels any chemistry."

"It would still be pretty sweet to have a friend who's gay in town, no matter what else might come of it."

"I guess that's true. I don't know. But this is so scary. I mean, I don't want to let myself like him and dream about him if there's no hope of anything more. But I'm not sure I can stop."

"But liking him and dreaming about him is the fun part. Watching him in the halls. Looking forward to talking to him."

"I'm already doing that, but I'm not so sure it's fun. It's pretty terrifying."

"That's okay. I was scared Ryan wasn't going to like me."

"Seriously? The guy is crazy about you. I'm pretty sure he was more scared that you wouldn't like him. The way I'm scared Benjamin could never like me."

"How can he not? You're smart, talented, and gorgeous! Those big brown eyes and that curly hair. Any guy would be lucky to have you!" I can see why Ryan's obsessed with her. She's beautiful *and* observant. Ha, ha.

"Yeah, well, if I liked girls, I'd be giving Ryan a run for his money."

"Listen to you, all flirty. Try some of that with Benjamin and he'll be all over you."

"Yeah, right. I have no idea if he's interested in me at all."

"He told you he wants to be friends."

"I guess. Listen, I'll let you go. But I really appreciate that you're talking to me about this stuff."

"No problem. I'm sure Lucas would weigh in on things if you're interested in his...unique perspective."

"You mean the gay perspective? Do you think that would help?"

"I'm not sure if that's what I mean. I just mean the Lucas perspective. Which might help but might also make you totally confused. My brother is an original."

"That's true. Anyway, thanks, Clare. I'll think about talking to him, and I will definitely talk to you again soon. If you don't mind, that is."

"I don't mind. I actually like it, so contact me anytime. Good luck."

"Thanks. Bye."

I close my laptop and sit for a minute staring at the wall. It's not a very interesting wall. Just green paint with a couple of hockey posters that my dad bought me. I'm not a fan of hockey. I prefer soccer, which I'm actually pretty good at. I'm fast and can dribble better than most guys I've played with. My dad thinks soccer is a sissy sport because it's non-contact. Figures.

I like the color green. But I like all the other colors as well. I'd like to paint this place into an abstract rainbow and accent it with pictures that mean something to me. I love artwork that shows how beautiful the world can be, like Degas' dancers or Van Gogh's sunflowers. Although, what I'd really like is a picture of a deer that looks a little like a dog.

seven

"So, is Benjamin walking home with us again?" Ryan asks as we head for the door after school.

"I don't know. I guess we'll find out when we get outside." My voice is calm and casual even though all of my insides are starting to vibrate like they've done every day for the past two weeks at the thought that he might be standing there waiting for us again.

"Ryan! Shit, man, I've been looking for you everywhere!" Cody runs up behind us.

"Really? Because I went to my locker and now, I'm going to the door so I can leave, which is what I do every day. Not sure where you were looking."

"Yeah, well, it isn't what you're supposed to be doing today. You are supposed to be at the pool. Remember? Extra practice for the meet this weekend? Coach is going to fry our asses for being late!" He grabs the handles of Ryan's chair and spins him around. He doesn't say anything to me. He mostly ignores me unless we're in the pool, which we don't do much these days because he's busy training and doesn't have time for me. I can swim pretty well now, so it's probably safer for me to practice on my own anyway.

"Shit. I did forget. I guess you're on your own, Jack," Ryan calls over his shoulder as Cody jogs down the hall, using the wheelchair as a battering ram on the way to the community pool, which is connected to the far end of the school.

I keep walking forward, wondering if I should slow down or speed up. Benjamin is used to having the two of us to talk to. How will he feel about me showing up alone? Maybe I should just wait until tomorrow when Ryan will be with me again. I might run out of things to say and then I'll bore him so much that we won't even be friends, let alone anything else.

Clare would tell me to calm down, get my ass outside, and just let it happen. Easy for her to say because she's always calm and never runs out of things to talk about. She's the queen of conversation.

By the time I finish trying to figure out what to do, I'm already at the door. And my heart feels like it literally stops beating.

He's just standing there, leaning against the railing. The sun is pouring down on his head, and he's smiling like a cat does when it's hanging out on a window sill. His eyes are closed, which is too bad because I imagine that they'd actually manage to shoot sparks in the sunlight today. His hair hangs down to his shoulders, all loose and sexy, because he always removes the elastic the minute he gets out of school. He told us he just uses it because his mom makes him.

He's wearing a black, knee-length coat, left open to show off his usual brightly colored shirt—purple today with a black collar—tucked into black jeans. Even though he definitely dresses different from the guys around here, every girl who walks by gives him several looks. Apparently, there aren't too many rumors yet about him being gay even though he doesn't really seem to be hiding anything, seeing as he already told Ryan and me—and who knows how many other people. Maybe he just hasn't been here long enough for the rumor mill to begin operating.

I open the door and step outside. He opens his eyes and grins as he sees me.

"Hey," he says, walking over to me. Now my heart feels like someone put high-voltage jumper cables into my chest and jolted it into an erratic rhythm that I'm sure must somehow show on my face.

"Hey." *Good comeback. Very original.*

"No Ryan today?" he asks, looking behind me. *Does he look disappointed?*

"No. Cody just snagged him for swim practice." *Snagged? What kind of word is that?*

"Cody. My mother's favorite student." He laughs.

"Yeah, Cody. He likes to drive admin crazy. There's a rumor that he actually drove St. Clair away."

"Really? Well, remind me to thank him some time." He gives me a look that makes everything inside of me start beating so fast that I feel like I might pass out.

"I hope he doesn't drive your mom too nuts," I manage to choke out, even though my throat has gone a bit dry. Like the Sahara on a hot day.

"Actually, Mom kind of likes the bad boys. She always says her job would be too easy if everyone behaved themselves. She used to teach a whole class of kids who had been kicked out of the regular school system and she loved it."

"Why'd she become a VP?"

"Money. Prestige. I don't know. She likes it well enough, although I think your buddy Cody might be the challenge that makes her go back to the classroom."

"Cody is no buddy of mine."

"Oh, no? I thought he and you and Ryan were all *besties*." He grins as he emphasizes the word.

"Ryan and I are…friends. But Cody and I barely tolerate each other. We accidentally went on a road trip together, but that's about it."

"*Accidentally* went on a road trip? That sounds like a story."

"Not much of one. Ryan invited me, and I didn't know Cody was going until I'd already said yes. I got pissed off at some ignorant comment Cody made when we were there and told him I'm gay, which scared the shit out of me at first but ended up having the positive effect of his mostly ignoring me when other people are around, so I don't soil his reputation."

I stop talking, surprised at how many words I just managed to string together. We're having a conversation and Ryan's not even here to keep it going!

"Oh, one of those." He nods.

"Yeah, one of many of *those* in this town."

"Hey, Jack. How are you doing?" The high-pitched, very obnoxiously flirty voice interrupts us. Sarah Edey is standing in front of me, smiling, which is something she has never done in my direction before. She has a couple of friends with her who have faces I recognize but names I forget.

"Um, fine." She smiles even more widely, until her face seems split in half by her big mouth. Her eyes shift from me to Benjamin.

"Who's your friend?" she asks, fluttering her eyelashes as if she got dirt in her eye and is trying to blink it out.

"Benjamin Lee, at your service," he says, with a bow that makes all of them giggle. I just roll my eyes. They're playing on the wrong soccer field.

"I'll just bet you are," Sarah says in what I assume she thinks is a seductive voice but mostly sounds silly.

"And you are?" he asks. Sarah tilts her head to one side. Maybe she has water in her ear.

"I'm Sarah. These two are Jillian and Samantha." Jillian and Samantha just wave.

"Nice to meet you, ladies. Hope I'll see you again sometime," Benjamin says politely, while at the same time making it clear the conversation is over.

"Oh, you will. Count on it!" says Sarah, sounding more

threatening than sexy as her two silent handmaidens nod. The three of them skip off, waving at us—at *Benjamin*—as they go.

"Does that happen to you a lot?" I ask Benjamin as we start walking again.

"What?"

"Girls flirting."

"Oh, yeah. Quite often. Does it happen to you a lot?"

"Never. I guess they can't tell with you." He looks at me curiously. "That you're gay, I mean," I finish, feeling a little self-conscious.

"No, I don't have it written on my forehead." He pushes his hair back and shows me. I smile, wondering if his hair feels as silky as it looks.

"Do your friends back home know?" I ask. He looks at me in surprise.

"That I'm gay? Of course, they do! Everyone knows. I don't hide who I am." Now I'm the one who's surprised.

"You're out? Like, completely?" Just like Caleb and Lucas, but he's so much younger. I had it in my head that coming out is something you do when you're older and it's...safer somehow.

"Pretty much. I mean, I don't announce it the minute I walk into a room."

"You told Ryan right away."

"If it comes up naturally, I don't hide it. I was asking Ryan what it's like to be the only guy in a chair, and that got us talking about being different, so it just came out in the conversation. Obviously, most people here haven't figured it out yet. At least, Sarah and her buddies don't seem to have."

"You might want to keep it that way while you're living here." He gets that curious look on his face again.

"Really? Why is that?"

"Because Thompson Mills is a few years behind the known universe in its acceptance level. Like about a century or two. I'm safer being the subject of rumors than admitting that at least one of them is actually true. There's a lot of serious homophobia around here."

"Serious how?"

"Serious as in I was pinned to a dumpster by a couple of gangbangers one time who wanted to flatten my nose so that I wouldn't start hitting on the local guys. They would have managed it, too, if Cody hadn't shown up and smacked them around a little."

"Your *not*-friend Cody?"

"Well, Ryan was there with me. Cody was mostly protecting him. Those guys were such asswipes that they would have punched out a guy in a chair. Until the swim team showed up and stopped them."

"The swim team? On TV it's always the football team that saves the day." Benjamin laughs, but I don't join him.

"I think you might want to reconsider being too open about it here. It's not like where you come from." He smiles at me and shakes his head slightly.

"Don't get me wrong. There are lots of homophobes and asswipes in the city too. It's definitely not all sunshine and roses. Maybe the difference is that there are also enough decent people floating around to balance things out a bit."

"Well, there isn't much balance around here. This town is so small that being different usually means you're flying solo. Take Ryan. He's the only guy outside of the nursing home who is in a wheelchair, so the school and the rest of the town aren't even fully accessible. And up until now, I'm the only gay guy I've ever heard of who lives here. I still hide it from everyone except about six people. I mean, I don't know the whole town, and maybe there are people who would accept me, but I wouldn't know where to find them. I'm too scared to try anyway." He nods, unconcerned at my big revelations.

"There are also probably other gay people you just haven't met yet."

"That doesn't help much. I can't exactly take out an ad looking for gay friends, can I?"

"Why not?" He grins a little.

"Because I'd get my ass kicked."

"Then obviously it's time for things to change."

"It's been time for a change as long as I've been living here, but it takes more than one person to change a whole town." *I sound like a bumper sticker.*

"You just said it's a very small town."

"Not small enough for me to make any difference."

"Nothing ever changes unless people are willing to try."

"You sound like you're on one of those after school specials my mother used to make me watch when I was little." I laugh at him and he smiles.

"Yeah, well those shows had to come from somewhere. Just because they're all hokey doesn't mean they aren't based on some kind of reality. I know I'm not willing to change myself for this or any other town. I worked hard to get to where and who I am. People will just have to deal with it."

I feel a quick stab of fear at the thought of what could happen if he goes around telling people he's gay. Then just as quickly, I get a pang of envy at the thought that he *wants* to go around telling people he's gay. The pangs and stabs give me a mess of mixed emotions that leave me speechless.

"So, I'm guessing you guys don't have a Pride parade here," he says after several seconds of silence. I look at him as if he just pointed out a unicorn walking down the street.

"You *are* kidding right?" I ask incredulously. The closest thing this town has had to a Pride parade was the time Lucas and Caleb came to visit me and walked down Main Street. And Lucas was in reverse drag, as he calls it, complete with jeans and a plaid shirt that he thought would make him fit in. Everyone still stared because they were strangers.

"I guess a little. But maybe that's what we should do."

'What?"

"Organize a Pride parade. I helped do the float from our school last year. It was cool."

"You think we should have a Pride parade in Thompson Mills? That would be exciting. You and me walking down Main Street while people throw things at us." *Like sticks and stones, not to mention a few names that will probably hurt me.*

"I think we could do better than that. I'm sure you have friends who would come. I have friends who would come from home. I bet Ryan would help. It would be amazing."

"It would be something. Not sure amazing is the right word for it."

"Well, I think we should talk about it some more. Not right now because I have to get home and study for that art history test that you could probably pass with your eyes closed."

He's right about the art history test. I read those books for fun. He is not right about Thompson Mills having a parade. My mother has come a long way from the day I came out to her, but I don't know if she'd ever come far enough to see me headlining a Pride parade. She would probably spend the rest of her life in church praying for my soul if I did anything that public. Just thinking about it makes my palms sweat—and not in a good way.

"See you later, Jackson. Go home and dream about rainbow flags and artistic parade floats!" Benjamin calls to me as he takes off toward home, probably looking to see if he can find any unicorns along the way.

eight

On that day last year when I finally got the guts to tell my mother who I am, everything completely blew apart, breaking me into so many pieces that I didn't think I could find them all and put myself back together.

I still have nightmares about standing in the living room trying to tell her what was going on in my life. Ryan was sitting there with me, trying to be supportive but probably wishing the floor would open up and swallow him while I tried to tell my mother how unhappy and confused I'd been feeling basically forever. I just about lost my courage when her eyes filled up with tears as I tried to explain how I ended up in the water that day. How I had felt so desperately tired of being afraid that I wanted to escape from everything, including myself. *Especially* myself.

That I was so terrified of hurting her, I didn't know what to do.

When I first started talking, Mom nodded sympathetically, as if she knew what I was going to say, and I had this flash of hope that maybe she did. That maybe she was going to tell me she'd known all along, like on that TV show *Glee*, where the gay kid comes out to his dad, and his dad says, "I've known since you were three," and they hug and everything is okay.

But our conversation was nothing like that.

It took about thirty seconds for me to realize that she thought I was upset because of the divorce. Like, somehow I'd been battered and bruised by her finding the courage to kick out the man who had made both our lives miserable. She thought I felt responsible for the breakup and that my guilt drove me into the river.

I wish I *had* been responsible for it. That would be something to be proud of.

Mom was trying so hard to be sympathetic and understanding that it made my head start to hurt like it was caught in a vise. I could feel the blood throbbing, pounding in my brain. I knew I had to get it over with before she said anything else. I had to just tell her before she came up with six other reasons to explain my messed up life.

My throat closed up every time I imagined saying it out loud. Two little syllables that choked me every time I tried to shake them loose.

Two little syllables that would change everything.

I'm gay.

I don't know how I finally managed to get the words out, but the second I did, I wanted to reach out and grab them so

I could shove them back down my throat. I was shaking so badly that the room vibrated and, at first, I couldn't focus on my mother's face. I was so afraid of what I was going to see written on it that I thought I was going to pass out before I got the shaking under control enough to actually see her.

I closed my eyes, trying to calm myself down. After a few seconds, I managed to risk opening them.

My mother was just sitting there, still and silent like a petrified version of herself, staring at me with no expression at all on her face. I understood in that moment what Ryan meant when he said that my eyes looked like black holes the first time he met me. My mother's eyes seemed dark and empty, reaching back to somewhere I didn't want to go.

I'd had enough nightmares about this moment that I thought I was prepared for the worst. That I'd be ready for whatever she said or did after I told her. I knew it could go really badly and that I had to be ready to deal with whatever happened.

But I wasn't ready for those empty eyes staring me into nothingness. And I wasn't ready when they filled up with tears as she came to life again and begged me to tell her it wasn't true. That I couldn't possibly be gay without her knowing it. That I had a girlfriend when I was twelve, so obviously I couldn't be gay. That she had spent my whole life believing I would grow up and marry a woman who would give her grandchildren.

Her son couldn't be gay. It was impossible!

She wanted me to agree with her. To tell her I was wrong and she was right. That I had made a mistake, and everything would be fixed if I just took it back and buried it where it belonged. And part of me wanted to do it. Just rewind the conversation ten minutes into the past and keep this secret to myself. To live a lie until I was old enough to get away and find out if there might be some truth somewhere else.

But I couldn't do it. The words were finally out, and I wasn't going to take them back.

She tried calm, rational persuasion, reminding me that her church would never approve of me, as if somehow that would be so desperately important to me that I could just decide to be someone else. I told her I wanted *her* approval. I didn't care about some stupid church.

And then she changed tactics and decided it wasn't my fault after all. That I had somehow been persuaded to *become* gay because of something I'd seen or read on the Internet. Somehow I had been duped into believing it would be so wonderful to be different from everyone around me that I had spent all of this time living a lie inside of my own mind. I was pretending to *be* gay instead of pretending *not to be*. She told me not to worry. She wouldn't stand by and watch me destroy my life. She was going to find a way to fix me.

Fix me. Like I was someone's broken cell phone headed for the dumpster behind my school.

She didn't listen when I tried to tell her that I'm not broken or sick or trying to hurt her. That I didn't *decide* to be gay. She didn't listen when I tried to tell her that this is just who I am. That pretending to be someone I'm not was destroying my life.

She just kept shaking her head and coming up with her own version of the truth, while my world started to disintegrate around me.

I remember begging her to understand me, accept me. I walked toward her with my hands stretched out as if I were three again and wanted to be picked up. She stopped talking and sat staring at me, like I was stranger who had invaded her living room. I tried to talk to her again, but she just shook her head, leaned forward, and burst into harsh hysterical sobbing, rocking back and forth, holding her arms tightly against her stomach, like something inside her was about to break.

The room suddenly felt unbearably hot as the air disappeared, taking my breath away with it. I was afraid if I stayed there one more second, I would either faint or start screaming and never stop.

So I ran out of the room, leaving Ryan alone with her, probably wondering what he was doing there and what the hell he was supposed to do next.

I was out the door and halfway down the street when the sky split open and started to pour rain down on my head, but I couldn't slow down. I just kept running until I found myself at the bridge.

I don't know why I ended up there. I just knew I couldn't be anywhere near my mother with her endless tears and plans to make me into someone I'm not.

Matthew thinks I was planning to jump in and finish the job I started in the spring. Ryan obviously thought that too, because he sent Cody there to stop me before coming himself.

I don't know if I was planning anything. I'm not sure I was thinking at all. I don't remember the details of those first few minutes on the bridge. My memories are a soggy mess of tears and rain that just swirl around inside my mind without sense or direction. All I know is that Cody kept grabbing me and Ryan kept talking to me until I wanted to throw both of them over the railing. I don't know how long the three of us were there before my mom showed up.

I found out later that Ryan called his mom before leaving for the bridge and she went straight over to my house so she could get my mom and bring her to us. Mrs. Malloy told me that when she got to my place, my mother was already out the front door and coming to find me. I hope that's true.

My mother came over to me and stood there, rain pounding down, plastering her hair to her skull and soaking through her thin sweater. She shivered a little as she reached over and put her arms around me, telling me she was sorry. She had been taken by surprise and she had reacted badly. She said she loved me and wanted me to come home so we could figure it out together.

I had no idea what she meant by that, but she was holding me and saying she loved me, and that was all that mattered. In that moment, it was enough to get me out of the rain.

My mother still comes and sits in on the first half hour of my counseling sessions with Matthew so that we can all talk about how we're going to "figure it out." After all these months, I don't know how much we have figured out. She is definitely trying really hard to understand that being gay isn't something

I just decided to try on like a new coat. She's also doing her best to get past her own lifelong belief that homosexuality is inherently wrong or evil. I guess she's trying to reconcile the teachings of the church that she loves with the realities of the son that she loves. But she's definitely not ready to head to a Pride parade, no matter what Benjamin would like to believe is possible in this town.

I know she's only lived with it for a few months, but it's obvious to me that she still wants to cry every time she actually has to say the word *gay*, which she only does when Matthew makes her. When Matthew and I are alone, he says that I have to be patient with her and give her time to join us here in the twenty-first century. That I have to try to understand where she's coming from and to recognize how far she's going to have to travel to get to where I am. So, I'm trying. But it's hard to wait sometimes. I feel like life is passing by too fast for her to keep up, and I'll be gone from home before she can fully accept me, and by then it'll be too late. Now that I've had the guts to tell her, I don't want to leave home next year and have to wonder if I'll be welcomed back.

The other thing Matthew tries to talk to me about is my father. He's been living in another town for months now and doesn't have any real idea what's been going on. He only knows that I had an accident in the river back in the spring and that Ryan jumped in and saved me. He doesn't know anything else. Matthew thinks it's a mistake to keep the truth from him, but I don't care what Matthew thinks. I actually don't care what my father thinks either, but I don't want to deal with whatever poison he would send my way if he knew that his son liked boys. And pretty clothes. And makeup.

Lucas would tell me I should put on a fabulous dress, find some matching lip gloss, and march right up to my dad and kiss him on the cheek.

It would probably give him a heart attack.

Maybe it's not such a bad idea after all.

nine

"So, I was wondering if you had time to help me with my art project."

Benjamin and I are walking home alone again because now Ryan has regular after-school swim practices, compliments of Coach Steve, who was not happy with the team's performance in the swim meet last week. At first I thought Benjamin might start coming up with excuses to avoid being alone with me three times a week, but he's here every day, waiting for me even if I'm a few minutes late. And every day my heart starts beating too fast and my stomach fills with really happy butterflies that seem to be spending their time dancing around in circles.

"The social slash personal thing?" Our term project in art class is to create a work of art in any medium we choose that reflects something of social significance that also has personal meaning for us. My art teacher has high hopes, I think. I haven't figured out what I'm going to do yet. It's not due for a while, so I'm not sure what Benjamin's worried about.

"Yeah, I want to get started soon. We're going home next weekend, and I won't have much time to work. Art isn't my strong subject, as you know, so I need to get started now."

"You're going home?" I ask, still not answering his question. I want to ask him if he has someone there waiting for him, but I'm afraid to. He did say he was looking for a date for grad, but he might have been just joking around. It doesn't mean he's actually single, does it?

"Oh, yeah. We have to be there for New Year's."

"Um, I hate to tell you this, but New Year's Eve was a month ago."

"Not that one. Chinese New Year. It's the big celebration in my dad's world. Sort of like your Christmas, my mom's Hanukkah, and December 31st all rolled into one, with a bit of Thanksgiving thrown in. Except seeing as there's no real Chinese community here, there wouldn't be the type of celebrating that my dad's used to, so we're going home. My grandparents are still living in our house, and we'll be staying there."

"They were living with you before you moved?"

"Yep. Ever since I was little. My dad sponsored their immigration right after I was born. They decided to stay behind when we came here because they have a lot of Chinese friends in the city. Dad and Mom decided to keep the house and just rent here because they weren't sure how long we'd be staying."

"My grandparents lived with us for a while when they first immigrated here, too. I was just a little kid when they moved out and we came here. They have their own place a couple of hours from here. I don't see them as much as I'd like to." I don't tell him the rest. That the only reason they don't still live with me is my father, who always made it clear he didn't want them around.

"Yeah, I miss my *Ye Ye* and *Nai Nai*."

"Mine are *Abuelito* and *Abuelita!*" We both laugh.

"Anyway, I've decided on a project. Sort of. But I need some creative input from you." He smiles hopefully.

"Sure. Anything you need." *Literally anything.*

"Well, after I told you to dream about rainbow flags, I started doing exactly that, and it came to me—it would make a great project."

"A rainbow flag?" Okay, so maybe not *anything.* These projects are the kind you present out loud and in front of everyone. Not the right crowd for rainbow flags.

"Well, a rainbow to symbolize the flag that actually symbolizes a rainbow. That's the artistic bit. I was thinking of using the image of a rainbow as a way to talk about the symbolism of the flag and its importance to the LGBTQ+ community."

I look at him to see if he's kidding. His eyes are serious but enthusiastic at the same time.

Is he nuts? That would be exactly like walking into the room and announcing that he's gay. As far as I know, no one else in our school would give the slightest shit about anything like rainbow flags or gay pride. Or gay anything. Unless they're using it as an insult.

"Bad idea? Not creative enough?" he asks, after I stand there staring with my mouth open for so long that he realizes I'm not going to take my turn.

"No, it sounds really creative. It's just…are you sure that's a good idea?"

"Well, no. That's why I'm asking you to help me. Maybe a rainbow is too hokey or something."

"No, rainbows are awesome. I love rainbows. They're beautiful and my favorite songs are about them." I'm babbling and he knows it. He starts to grin.

"That's good! Then you should also like rainbow flags and what they stand for."

"I do, but I'm not sure too many other people care. If you do a project on this, everyone will decide you're gay because they'll figure someone straight would never do something like that."

"I *am* gay."

"But if you announce it to the whole class by doing this project, it'll spread like crazy and *everyone* will know. Then it won't be safe for you." He looks at me seriously, shaking his head.

"It can spread wherever it wants to. I'm not hiding who I am. I told you that before. I guess there are different kinds of safe. I don't feel safe pretending to be someone I'm not."

"And I think trying to hide it is the only thing that keeps me…relatively safe."

"Well, we can agree to disagree, I guess." He shrugs. He seems disappointed in me, and my stomach drops down to my feet as I scramble around inside my brain trying to find a way to fix this.

"I can help you. Just…promise me you'll be careful. Stay away from dumpsters and don't go too many places alone. I think that most of the jerks around here are all talk, but there's always someone willing to use his fists to make a point." *Please don't let anyone break that beautiful nose or bruise those gorgeous eyes.*

"Well, talking can't hurt me, and I'm pretty good at dealing with fists too." He flexes his bicep and I feel a couple of butterflies doing cartwheels. "So, rainbows. Kind of a basic concept. I need something brilliant."

"Okay. Um, let me think. Do the colors on the flag have any particular meaning?" I ask, hoping the butterflies don't cartwheel their way into my voice.

"They do. I actually looked it up last night to get started on my research. There are two ways to explain it. One, that the blend of different colors represents harmony and acceptance of all the different people of the community, and, two, that each color has a specific meaning."

"Like what?"

"Just a sec. I have them listed on my phone." He digs his phone out of his pocket and brings up the list. "Okay, it was slightly different depending on which site you're on, but basically the short version is that red is for life; orange is for healing; yellow is sunlight; green, nature; blue, harmony and peace; and purple is for the spirit. That's today's flag. There used to be two other colors—hot pink for sex and turquoise for magic."

I imagine a watercolor rainbow stretching across a canvas or bristol board or whatever Benjamin decides to use. I try to envision some brilliant way to make meaning out of the simple stripes.

"You could create the different stripes out of words that reflect the meaning of the color. Either just repeat the one word over and over in all different shapes and sizes or come up with synonyms or something? Even phrases or poems. Song lyrics. Anything. Although I'm not sure you should include hot pink in a school project." Not sure our art teacher is ready for repeated versions of the word *sex* in a class presentation.

Benjamin smiles widely and nods.

"I knew you'd come up with something. And the brilliance of it all is that I don't even have to draw anything but a bunch of lines."

"Which isn't quite as easy as it sounds. You have to get the proportions right so that it actually looks like a rainbow. I can help you outline the rainbow, and you can do the rest. I've drawn a million of them. When I was a kid, every painting I made had one floating around in it. Every time I draw one, I hear 'Somewhere over the Rainbow' in my head." I laugh a bit self-consciously. I never told anyone that before.

"Judy Garland was an icon to the gay community. Some people even think she was part of the reason the rainbow flag ended up being used."

"She was totally amazing, but I also like Harry Nilsson's version. It's in my key."

"Never even heard of the guy. I'd like to hear you sing it for me some time."

"Maybe. I mostly sing to my mirror." I'm not sure I'd remember any of the words if Benjamin was looking at me.

"If you sing anywhere near as well as you draw, you must be great."

"Not really. I took a few lessons but quit a long time ago. Do you think I love rainbows because I'm gay?"

"You probably love them because you're artistic and love color." He laughs.

"Maybe I like singing about them because I'm gay."

I'm gay. Every time I say the words out loud to him, I feel a little tingle in my brain, like that feeling you get when someone gives you a really nice compliment and you feel…well, all tingly and proud of yourself so that you have the sudden urge to run to a mirror to see if you somehow look different from how you did before.

"That might be true." He touches me on the shoulder and stands up.

"I guess I'd better get moving. My mom is having Principal Williams over for supper tonight, which is gross on so many levels."

"That *is* gross!" I can still feel the sensation from his hand on my shoulder, and I have to resist the urge to touch it.

"Yeah, well maybe I should get you an invite so you can suffer too."

"No thanks. I'd rather eat Char Char's burgers at the Supe."

He laughs and touches my shoulder again, feather light and quick. Everything inside of me starts a slow burn as if he just lit a match on my shoulder blade.

I stand there smoldering as I watch him leave, wondering if he knows I'm lying. I can't think of anything I'd like better than being invited to his house or anywhere else in the known universe so long as he's going to be there too.

ten

The next few weeks pass by much too fast. Benjamin did his Chinese New Year's trip home, and I really wanted to ask him if he saw any old boyfriends while he was there. But I didn't. Ryan asked me to come to Bainesville for Valentine's Day the following weekend, so I could see everyone while he visited Clare, but I said no because I thought Benjamin might call and ask me to come over and help him with his project on the weekend, seeing as it was due a week later. But he didn't.

He *has* been filling me in on the progress he's been making on the project that is going to change life as he knows it in Thompson Mills. He's been running ideas past me, and last night he practiced his speech with me over the phone. He also tried talking some more about the idea of a Pride parade here, and I keep trying to figure out a way to tell him no, without disappointing him at the same time.

81

He might stop talking about it after today though.

It's Art Project Day.

Mine is on the effects of immigration on communities and vice versa. I did a collage of my own drawings as well as photographs from the Internet, showing faces of people who came here from all different countries. I drew my own grandparents as part of it, explaining that they are the reason this is personal to me. Benjamin gave me pictures of his grandparents as well, which was cool. I used a map outline of our region as a background, which was meant to be somewhat ironic seeing as we are still basically homogenous here. A lot of people who move to this country seem to end up in urban areas where there are support systems in place and job possibilities. I was trying to say that we need to offer those same opportunities here so that we create some kind of diversity in small towns. I don't know if I managed it or not. I suppose my grade will tell me that.

I guess Benjamin's project is about diversity as well, only an even less popular version of it, in this neck of the woods, anyway. He showed me his finished project, and it's actually really good. Better than good. Fantastic. He decided to create something much more interesting than our original design. Taking the outline I made for him, he traced it onto a sheet of plywood, which he cut out with his mom's jigsaw. Instead of just painting words on the outline, he made the color bands out of different sizes and shapes of stones, painting them in various shades of each color and writing the words on the largest surfaces. He did a combination of repeating the core meaning of each color and adding other words that support it. His red section had "Life" a whole bunch of times, but also words like *birth* and *children* and *grow*. And *love*.

The result is this amazing three-dimensional, incredibly tactile rainbow that Benjamin can barely carry by himself, even with his impressive muscle tone. It's almost as wide as he is tall and weighs a lot, but it looks great and makes me wish I had spent more time on my own project.

"So, are you ready?" he asks me as we come into the room. His project is at the back of the room on a shelf because it's too heavy for the easel at the front. He has a detailed report neatly typed out in a folder beside it in case anyone in the class wants to take a look and learn a little more about the symbolism of the rainbow flag. *As if.*

"Ready as I'll ever be," I answer, not sure if he's asking if I'm ready to present my work or ready to see him do his. Either way, I'm lying.

"I hope the superglue holds," he says, grinning cheerfully. "I'd hate for the whole thing to disintegrate in the middle of my awesome speech. Your poster looks terrific."

"Not compared to your stone rainbow. It's beautiful, Benjamin. Really creative."

"Thanks. I wanted it to stand out a little. Wake people up when they see it."

"I don't think you have to worry about standing out today." I sigh a little as I head over to my desk. He seems so happy with himself. I hope everyone isn't as supremely shitty to him as I'm expecting them to be once the point of his speech gets pushed into their little minds.

The teacher makes us go in alphabetical order, which means Benjamin is about three people before me. I sit through the endless boring explanations of completely unimportant moments in history, my stomach starting to churn a little more energetically as each passing second brings Benjamin's moment of truth closer. I check to see if he's as nervous as I am, but he's just sitting there like he's actually paying attention to everyone's work and enjoying it.

"All right, thank you, Susan. Benjamin Lee," the teacher says in a voice that sounds more bored than she likely realizes.

Benjamin heads to the back of the room and stands by his project. There are a couple of snickers before he starts to talk, which doesn't bode well. Are rainbows inherently funny for some reason or has the rumor mill already started again?

"My project represents the rainbow flag, which is an important symbol within the LGBTQ+ community. The rainbow flag has become one of the most universally recognized flags in the world, reaching beyond national borders and uniting people of different cultures. It is a symbol of the struggle for acceptance and the celebration of unity and pride. The rainbow represents harmony within the diversity of the community, with each color holding its own specific meaning. I used stones as my medium because they're totally natural, just like my topic…which has personal meaning to me because I'm gay…and proud of it."

He just spits it out like a grape seed, ignoring the instant buzz in the room as he continues on to explain the different words he's used and why he chose them. He then goes into a bit more detail about the meaning of the different colors and how important the flag has become in the Pride movement. It's all really interesting, at least to me, but I've heard it before, and I can't stop myself from looking around the room as his voice disappears into a faint murmur that blends in with the buzzing in the room and the roaring that's started in my ears.

Some students are just sitting there, watching with glazed looks on their faces that mean they aren't as impressed with his stone rainbow as I am and are probably not even listening. Others are whispering to each other and staring at Benjamin instead of his project. A few people are staring at me instead of him, pointing in my direction and making I-told-you-so faces. Some of the girls are watching him and looking like they're going to cry.

Shit. This is going to be bad. Why did I let him do this? I should have been a better friend. I should have found a way to make him stop before he started.

After ten minutes that seem like ten times that many, the teacher thanks him for sharing his project in exactly the same way she thanked everyone else. She doesn't seem to see anything monumental in the fact that he just came out to the entire class. She asks if anyone has questions, but everyone just sits there staring at him, so he sits down, smiling at me as he passes. That starts the whispers and pointing all over again, and it occurs to me that I've been so worried about the effect this might have on Benjamin that I didn't realize it would bleed over onto me as well. People aren't blind around here. Everyone knows that we've become friends. Now they're going to decide that we're a couple. Two gay guys sitting in a tree.

I might not mind being officially "outed" by Benjamin's art project if we actually were a couple. I think I could stand up to pretty much anything if we were together.

"That went great, don't you think?" Benjamin asks as we walk out of the room at the end of class. He seems completely oblivious to Jonathan Avery walking behind us saying "Hey fag" in a soft voice that's just loud enough for us to hear, but not loud enough for the teacher.

"You did a good job," I say, as I try to shut out the eyes and fingers and voices.

"Yeah, *fag*, you did a good job," Jonathan says, increasing his volume as we get farther from the classroom. He laughs as if he's said something funny, and a couple of his friends join in.

"Why didn't you make a rainbow too, Jackie?" This time it's Peter Bronman. I ignore him, but he won't let it go. He comes up beside me and shoulder bumps me. "I asked you a question, gay boy."

Benjamin stops walking suddenly and turns to Peter. He stands there for a second, staring. He's a least four inches taller and probably outweighs him by fifty pounds of muscle. He just stares unflinchingly, arms folded with one hand loosely curled into a fist. After a few seconds, Peter makes an *I'm-too-cool-for-this* face and steps back. He probably figured out that it's not a good idea to get in a fist fight with a *fag* who looks like he can kick ass.

"Stupid queer," he says, shaking his head at Jonathan as the two of them take off to find someone else to vomit their ignorance on.

"Well, queer, fag, and gay. Quite the vocabulary for small-town assholes," Benjamin says pleasantly and quite loudly. A couple of people standing near us laugh. I look over at them and I'm surprised to see that they're looking at Benjamin as if they actually think he's funny.

"It isn't going to end there," I tell him.

"I don't expect it to. But they can't hurt me if I don't let them. That's one thing I've learned. You need to learn it too, I think."

"They can hurt you if they punch you."

"Well, that's debatable too. But I'll avoid letting anyone punch me just in case. You worry too much."

"But what if...?"

"Don't worry about me. I can take care of myself. Are you okay?"

"Me?"

"Yeah, I just realized that by hanging out with me, it's going to make all those rumors about you go into hyperdrive. So, if you want me to back off for a bit, I will."

"No!" The word shoots out so fast that he almost has to duck. He smiles as I turn every shade of red that he used on his rainbow. "I mean...you don't have to. We're friends, and it's no one's business but ours. And if they want to think I'm gay, let them."

The words come out strong and fearless.

I think I might have to go throw up now.

"That's good. I'm proud of you. I'm proud of me too. I think I'm going to get an A on that one. See you after school."

He heads off into the crowds changing classes, not the slightest bit worried that his life in this school has just changed for the worse.

"Hey!" Ryan comes wheeling up beside me.

"Hi."

"So I hear you had an interesting art class."

"Word travels fast. Class ended like three seconds ago."

"Long enough to get a few texts out and about. Sounds like Benjamin's more or less decided to tell everyone he's gay. And is bringing you along for the ride."

"It looks that way."

"Are you okay?" he asks, the hint of worry in his voice instantly putting me on the defensive until I realize that I just did exactly the same thing to Benjamin.

"Yeah, I think I am. I mean, I don't know how much will change for me. The rumors have been running around so long that most people have already decided anyway. Maybe they'll stop thinking I'm a perverted drug addict who robs banks and just stick with thinking I'm gay."

"I still think you're a perverted drug addict."

"Good, someone has to know the real me."

Ryan laughs at me and then sobers up quickly when he sees Cody coming toward us.

"Oh, man, I wonder if Cody's heard yet. He was telling me last week that he was going to ask Benjamin if he can swim because he noticed how big his shoulders and arms are. Cody's going to freak out six ways from Sunday when he finds out Benjamin's gay. He still hasn't got over finding out about you!"

"That's true. Maybe we should ask him if he wants to give Benjamin swimming lessons too. He could start a gay swim school. He'd be known as the Gay Coach. A happy little swim coach who's opened his heart to anyone who wants to find his way across the swimming pool." I smile sweetly as Cody reaches us. I'm not sure if he heard what I said or not, but he doesn't look happy. Which I have to confess, makes me extremely happy.

"What the hell? He's gay? I've been making comments about the guy's shoulders and he's gay?"

"Don't worry, Cody. I don't think it's catching."

"First you. Now him. It's like an epidemic."

"Definitely. We know two gay guys out of like two hundred plus guys in this school. Definitely taking over." Ryan shakes his head.

"There could be more guys who just haven't admitted it yet though, Ryan. Maybe Benjamin will start a trend," I say seriously.

Ryan nods. "That could happen. You guys should start a club."

"Actually, Benjamin said there is a rainbow club at his old school."

"Shut up! Both of you. This is so not funny." Cody looks like he wants to climb the walls.

"Actually, Cody. I wasn't trying to be funny. There is a club at Benjamin's old school, and maybe there should be one here too. I'll sign you up." I wave good-bye to Ryan and head off to my locker, leaving Cody sputtering away while Ryan alternates between ignoring him and laughing at him.

Rainbow flags. Rainbow clubs. And according to Benjamin, a rainbow parade.

Thompson Mills isn't going to know what hit it.

But what worries me is wondering when it's going to hit back.

eleven

"This is a relatively horrible time to be out of bed." Benjamin rubs his eyes and then blinks a few times, trying to wake up. He looks like an adorable little kid, and I just want to pick him up and hug him. Except that he's significantly taller than me and those muscles definitely make him heavier too. Not to mention the fact that this…relationship? friendship?…doesn't include hugging.

"I know. But it's the only time you can have this place more or less to yourself. Ryan shows up sometimes too, but I think he has morning practice today."

"Why would he come here at…" he checks his phone "…five fifty-three in the morning?"

"Mostly I think for the same reasons as me. He comes here early just to look at the river and think without anyone in the way." *Which is why I'm standing here right now, still alive and breathing.*

"I hope I'm not in your way then." He leans on the railing and stares out over the water, shivering a little in the early morning cold. I want to put my arm around him and warm us both up. Clare would probably tell me to go for it, but there's no way I'm ready to make that bold a move. I'm thinking I was pretty brave just inviting him here.

"If you were, I wouldn't have asked you to come. Obviously, you wouldn't have decided to wander out here this early on your own." He laughs and rubs his eyes again. Seriously adorable.

"Any minute now, I'll wake up enough to actually appreciate it. I can see why people like this town now that I'm standing here. It is gorgeous. The bridge seems pretty old though. It could use a paint job." He's right. The paint is almost gone now, with what's left on the aging wood slowly weeping off in tiny, faded red tears that end up in the river.

"It's been here as long as the town. I don't think it's been painted the whole time I've been living here."

"How long has that been?"

"Oh, since I was pretty small. Twelve years, give or take."

"That's a long time to live in a place that you don't feel like you fit into. Must have been hard." He takes a stone and tries to skip it across the water, but we're too high up and it just drops and disappears.

"I guess so. Some days are harder than others." I gaze down at the water, remembering, in spite of myself. I imagine what it looked like to Ryan sitting up here watching me that day. I can almost see the yellow skirt floating just below the surface as the rest of me disappeared from his view. What I can never imagine, no matter how many times I try, is how he got himself down there in time to drag me out and save me.

"Do you mind talking about it?" I blink a couple of times at Benjamin who is watching me closely and reading either my face or my mind.

What the hell is wrong with me?

It.

He doesn't have to explain what he means. Why did I bring him here, where *it* happened? This bridge is such a swirling mass of emotions for me, all blending together until I don't know where one starts and the other ends. I don't know why I thought I could just come here and pretend it's some kind of a happy place for me. I *do* love looking at the water. It *can* calm my insides and help me to think. But it also reminds me of the times in my life when thinking wasn't enough, and I literally took things too far. What made me think I could hide that from Benjamin?

Matthew says it's good to think about it. To remember and understand my own feelings. But it is so much harder to do than it sounds. Sometimes I feel like there's more than one of me in here—Jack and Jackson coexisting, each of us just watching and trying to figure out what the other one is doing and why. One of me standing on the bridge watching while the other tries to escape.

I know that Benjamin has heard the story of Ryan's rescue

by now. He's never mentioned it to me before though. Before I brought him to the scene of the crime.

"I don't know if I mind. I don't really talk about it much unless my counselor or my mother makes me." *Great. Now you just told him you're getting your already tiny head shrunk. Another rumor confirmed.*

"That's fine. I don't want to intrude. I just want you to know that you can talk to me if you want to. I've been fairly lucky because my family always accepted me, and so did most of my friends, but I still know what it feels like to be shit on by jerks for who I am."

"Especially since you moved here!" Things haven't improved in the weeks since Art Project Day. They aren't particularly worse either, which I guess is the glass half full way to look at it. Mostly just insults and a few hopefully empty threats now and then. At least that's all I've heard at school. It probably helps that Benjamin's mom is the VP. Gives him a bit of a protective bubble.

I really thought that my friendship with Benjamin was going to make rumors turn to instant reality, which would make it open season on me, but it doesn't seem to be happening. Nothing feels that different for me.

No, that's not true. *Everything* feels different. It's not just me now. It's both of us, which probably sucks for Benjamin who was being stalked by adoring crowds when he first came but now is followed by jerks who get their personal thrills trying to make other people feel like shit. *Trying* is the operative word here, because it really doesn't seem to work. Nothing these people come up with seems to bother Benjamin one bit. It all seems to bounce off the bubble and just float up into the atmosphere.

It doesn't suck for me though. When I'm with him, I feel like his bubble is big enough for two.

"It's not that bad. Not great either." He smiles briefly but then turns serious. "There were moments back home too. And not everyone I know has had an easy ride. I lost a friend a couple of years ago." He says the last sentence quickly, staring down at the water, biting his lower lip and gripping the railing tightly.

"Lost?" I ask, even though I'm fairly sure I know what he means.

"He was from a family that was having trouble accepting the idea that he was gay. They didn't kick him out but they didn't exactly throw a party. His dad was pretty brutal about the whole thing, made fun of him and told him he just needed to man up. That kind of shit." His grip tightens until his knuckles turn white. I stand there quietly. I'm not sure I want to hear the rest, but I don't want to tell him to stop either.

"He seemed really angry and depressed at first but then he said he was okay—that he didn't need his stupid father anyway. He started going in the opposite direction, partying really hard and acting like nothing in the whole world mattered but having a good time. It didn't feel…*right,* I guess, but he said he was fine. He got pissed when we tried to talk to him, so eventually we stopped and just let it go. We just let it go." He whispers the last part as he closes his eyes.

"One day he didn't show up at school. We didn't think much of it because he'd been skipping a lot of classes anyway. It wasn't until later that we found out that he was dead. Hanged himself in his garage."

Benjamin wipes his eyes, shaking his head angrily.

"They said he had lots of problems. That he had been angry and depressed for years. That maybe he was doing drugs. Stealing stuff. His parents blamed everything in the world. They were willing to let everyone think their kid was a drug addict and a thief. But they still couldn't admit he was gay—that being gay and feeling like he didn't belong in his own family had anything to do with what happened."

He smiles. It's the saddest expression I think I've ever seen, and my eyes start to sting in sympathy.

"I'm so sorry." It's all I can think of to say. Empty words that mean nothing.

"Me too. And I'm not trying to upset you by telling you about it. I just wanted you to know that I do get it. I don't live in a fantasy land where being gay is easy. It *should* be. I don't know why it isn't. Why would anyone care who I decide to spend time with? Who I want to love? It shouldn't be so hard that anyone feels like they can't be here anymore."

I turn my eyes back to the river. My mind instantly jumps down into the water again, to that moment when I felt like I just wanted it to take me away from here. From everywhere. I never wanted to stop floating, drifting off into some kind of oblivion that took away the fear of what my life was going to be when my mother and everyone else found out the truth…

or even worse, what my life would have to be if I could never tell. I take a deep breath. It catches in my throat for a second before I can make myself speak.

"I wanted to disappear. I didn't want to deal with it anymore. I just couldn't face one more day of lying and pretending. Except I'm still doing it. I tell Matthew that I don't know what I was thinking. I tell my mother that I was trying to get back to shore. That I was glad Ryan came when he did and saved me. But I wasn't. I *hated* him. I didn't think he saved me at all. The water was saving me, and he pulled me out. He sent me back!" The words are out of my mouth and floating out onto the water before I fully realize that I'm actually saying them out loud to Benjamin instead of to myself. I start to tremble and I'm not sure if it's from the cold or the realization that I just told the most amazing guy in the world that the rumor about me wanting to drown myself is true.

"You look cold," he says, putting one arm around my shoulders and rubbing my arm. I start shaking even harder and then totally mortify myself by starting to cry.

Benjamin pulls me into a full hug, wrapping his arms around me tightly the way my mother did on this same bridge that day in the rain. Except that this feels a whole lot different from being hugged by my mom. Even through the tears and total mortification, I can feel my stomach starting it's *oh-my-god-Benjamin-is-here* dance, amplified a million times because this time he's not just here. He's holding me and rubbing my back.

"I'm sorry." My voice is muffled against his chest. I'm probably wiping snot all over his jacket.

"Don't you dare say that! You have nothing to be sorry for. You're still here. You should be proud of yourself. You're getting through it."

"I still need a counselor every week to tell me what to think and I haven't told my dad and I worry about my mom and—"

"*So. What.*" The words come out, loud and clipped, almost like he's pissed. I stop my whining for a second and lean back.

"What?"

"I said, so what? So what if you need to see a counselor? Lots of people need someone to help them figure shit out. And if your dad deserves to be told, you'll figure out a way. And your mom? Man, she looks at you like she thinks you're the best thing on the planet. She loves you." He steps back out of the hug and just stands there looking at me. I feel cold. I wonder if he'll notice if I start trembling again.

"I think she still believes I'm going to hell." I mutter it, sounding like a three-year-old who's pissed he didn't get chocolate sauce on his ice cream. Benjamin just laughs.

"Maybe she just needs more time. Besides, I think my mother believes that about me sometimes too, but not because I'm gay. And she'd never admit it, but I *know* my mother thinks that Cody kid is going to hell. She might even help send him there." Now I start to laugh, hiccupping and sniffing at the same time. I probably have crap all over my face, and my eyes likely look like my dad's after a bender.

"I'd be happy to give him the final push down. The guy has tried to drown me about a dozen times in the past six months."

"*Drown* you?"

"Yeah, he started giving me swimming lessons after…" I just point down at the river. Benjamin nods.

"Well, I'm glad you've been taking lessons, but I'm surprised they'd be from Cody."

"He's actually the best swimmer at school, and besides, Ryan's always been there too."

"That's better. You guys are good friends."

I look at him considering. "Mostly."

He seems a bit surprised by my answer but doesn't ask me to explain, so I don't bother saying anything else. My issue with Ryan is something I need to figure out with him, I think.

"Anyway, Jack, I hope you don't think I came down here to do some kind of amateur therapy session. I *was* just coming to see the water with you. The rest just kind of…happened."

"It's fine. I obviously needed to talk about it." I can still feel the echo of his arms wrapped around me, his hand rubbing my back.

"Well, I don't know how helpful it would be, but you can talk to me about anything. Anytime."

"Thanks. And I did bring you here just to look at the water and see my thinking spot. Maybe we could try again sometime and just enjoy the view."

"Sounds like a plan. So, I guess we should go home and get ready for school."

"I guess so. See you in class." I take a quick peek up at him, but he's already walking away.

I stay for a few seconds after he disappears from view,

trying to calm my insides down enough so that my outsides don't start joining in again. No point in starting the whole trembling and shaking routine if no one is here to hold me and make it go away.

I can't believe I got so personal with him! Telling him things I haven't even told Matthew or my mom. Things I haven't even told myself in a very long time.

I don't know if I just made us closer or if I scared him away.

twelve

"Were you at the bridge?" My mom is standing in the front hall when I get in, arms folded, face unreadable.

"Yes. I just needed some thinking time." I try to keep the irritation out of my voice.

"Was Ryan with you?" she asks.

"No!" The word comes out louder than I meant it to, but I hate it when she gives me the third degree, and I hate it worse that somehow she thinks I need to have Ryan with me whenever I go to the bridge.

"So, you were alone?" She makes it a question. Her face says that the answer is going to matter, but I'm not sure why. I have a quick internal debate over whether or not to tell her that Benjamin was there. I have a feeling that she would not see him as a valid replacement for Super Ryan.

"No. Benjamin came with me." I'm tired of lying. Hiding.

Whatever you want to call it.

"You two are becoming quite close." She stares at me. I don't think I like what I see in her eyes.

"He's my friend. Like Ryan is." I don't know why I added that. Legitimizing Benjamin in my mother's eyes by equating him with Ryan is not fair.

"Is he?" She folds her arms, tapping her fingertips on her elbow. It's a familiar pose, the one she used to use when I was little and she knew I was lying about something, like whether or not I snuck a cookie before supper.

"Yes. Is there a problem here? Is there something you want to say about Benjamin?" I sound tough, but my insides are starting to shake. I don't want to do this with her. I don't want to hear that she doesn't want me around Benjamin because the whole town probably knows he's gay by now. I don't want to know that she still wishes her son wasn't gay, even though she says she's cool with it when she's trying to impress the counselor.

I *don't* want to do this, but I'm going to. I have to. I fold my own arms and stand my ground, doing my best to stare her down.

She breaks eye contact, looking over my shoulder at the front door, as if it might have the answer written on it.

"People are talking about him. About you. At the restaurant." *I knew it.*

"I'm not surprised. And?" *Here it comes.*

"And they're saying that he's gay. And that you're gay. And that the two of you are…" She lets the sentence trail off as if the words are just too difficult to say. Or maybe she just doesn't know what word to use when you're talking about a *couple* that happens to be gay.

"I wish!" The words pop out unplanned, and her eyes whip back to mine.

"You wish? You wish for people to talk about you all over town?" Her voice is strained. I take a deep breath.

"No. Actually, I wish people would find something else to talk about. I wish people would leave me the hell alone and leave Benjamin the hell alone! I wish everyone had a brain in this town and could understand that it takes more than one kind of person to make a world. And I wish that I lived anywhere in that world but goddamn Thompson Mills!" I'm yelling by now and I don't care.

"Jackson, you watch your language!"

"No, Mom. *You* watch *your* language. You stand there waiting for me to come home, all concerned. But not worried that something happened to me. Worried that some*one* happened to me. Well, someone did. And he's great. He has been nothing but nice to me from day one. He's someone I care about and who means something to me. Someone I wish I could mean something more to than just a friend. He's never hurt anyone in this stupid town. And all you can say to me is that you're worried about what people—ignorant, stupid people—are saying about me and my friend."

She turns away abruptly and goes to sit down in the living room. I stay where I am.

"Jack. *Mi corazón.* Come, sit with me. I'm doing this all wrong. Once again." When my mom is emotional, the Spanish that she worked so hard to hide from my father comes back. She rubs one hand over her eyes and then tries a shaky smile. I'm confused. I thought we were about to have a big fight. Did I win already?

I come and sit down beside her on the couch. She reaches over and takes my hand, rubbing her thumb across the back of it as she speaks.

"I'm afraid that you'll be hurt. *More* hurt. The…talking had slowed down for a while. Then when *this boy* arrived, it all started up again. About him and about you. I worry about how it will affect you. And I'm afraid that you will get hurt."

"I'm not going to let the words get to me this time. I'm sick of other people being allowed to mess up my life with their ignorance. Benjamin is teaching me that."

"Matthew tried to tell you that many times."

"But he never lived it, I don't think. Benjamin is gay. Like me. He comes from a really different type of world than I do, but he's still had to deal with his share of shi…stuff." Mom smiles and touches my cheek.

"You have…feelings for this boy?"

"Yes. I do."

She nods, trying so hard to be understanding instead of horrified that I can't help smiling at her.

"It's okay, Mom. I know this is hard for you to hear. But that's kind of what this is all about. My feelings. When I have them for someone else, it's going to be a boy. That's the whole gay bit."

"*Lo sé!*" she says indignantly. "Of course, I know. Young

hearts break easily." She puts one hand gently on my chest in the general region of my heart. "I don't know if you are strong enough to handle it if he doesn't...have feelings for you. Does he? Do you know?"

I look at her in something close to shock. Is this real? My mother is not upset because he's a guy—she's upset because she doesn't want my heart to get hurt?

"No, I don't really know how he feels. Not yet anyway. But I know that this stuff doesn't always work out. You don't have to worry. I'm ready for whatever happens." I think. I hope.

"*Mi querido niño.* No one is ever ready for heartbreak. And you have had such trouble already." She sniffles a little as she puts her arm around me.

"I'm okay. I'm not going to do anything stupid if this doesn't work out. I know it might not. But I'll figure it out. I have friends to talk to. Matthew is there, all up in my face once a week. And I have you." Her eyes lock onto mine again, and she gazes into me for so long that I start to feel like she's actually in there wandering around, reading my mind.

"You do have me. Always and forever. You do understand that now, right? I will never let you walk away from me again. I am your mother. *Te amo.*"

"*Si, mama. Te amo también.*"

And she folds me into a hug that feels almost as good as the one Benjamin gave me on the bridge.

Almost.

"I have to go do some work before school," I tell her, to break the hug. She always buys that one.

"Of course. I'll make you some breakfast in a bit."

"I'm not…" I almost tell her not to bother, but then I realize that making me some food is probably something she's doing for herself as much as for me. My mother likes to see people eat. Comfort food. Guess she picked the right career. "Sure, that would be great." She gives me a kiss and a smile on her way to the kitchen as I go down to my bedroom.

I pick up my phone, checking the time and wondering if it's a bad time to bug Clare. She's probably getting ready for school by now and won't appreciate my whining in her ear about Benjamin first thing in the morning.

If she's busy, she can just ignore me though, right? Pretend she didn't notice me?

"Hey, Jack. You're up early." She answers immediately, and I suddenly feel embarrassed calling her.

"Yeah, sorry. I should have waited until after school to bother you."

"I told you before—you don't bother me."

"You aren't sick of my sad little love life?" I try a self-deprecating smile.

"Not at all. My friend Sherry talks to me about hers every day, for about two hours. It's a relief to talk to someone different and less…wordy." She laughs.

"Yeah, well, that's kind of why I'm calling. I got so wordy today that I'm afraid I messed up." I cringe, thinking about my outburst on the bridge.

"With Benjamin, I'm assuming?"

"Yes. We were on the bridge today."

"Oh." She looks surprised for a second but then nods slightly. "Okay. You were on the bridge, and...?"

"We just got talking about...life, I guess, and all of a sudden I was babbling like an idiot and telling him everything about *that* day, and I ended up saying things I'd never said out loud before. Personal, personal stuff that he probably doesn't need, or want, to hear from me this early in whatever it is we are to each other."

"Getting personal is part of being friends."

"Not this personal. I mean, I know he'd have heard about Ryan pulling me out of the water because it was news or whatever. And I know he heard the rumors that I was trying to...kill myself. But I didn't want that to be who I am to him. I wanted to be something...*someone* different to him. Shit, I don't know what I'm trying to say here."

"That's okay. Just take your time."

"We don't have much time seeing as we both have to go to school."

"School can wait." Clare gives me an incredibly gentle smile that reaches into my scrambled mind and helps me calm down a little. I take a deep breath and then try to push the words out in a way that makes sense.

"It's just...my whole friendship with Ryan has always been so weird because of the 'superhero rescues the weak victim' routine."

"No one thinks you're weak, Jack."

"That's not true. Ryan does. Cody does. Most of the school does. I'm seen as the weak little guy who couldn't handle my own shit and decided to take a header off the bridge, even though I actually walked into the water, a little fact that no one seems to care about. Anyway, regardless of how I got in there, everyone knows I did it. If your boyfriend hadn't been there, I probably would have drowned."

"If that had happened, it would have been terrible. Beyond." She shudders a little.

Right after it happened, I thought the terrible thing was that I didn't drown. That I had to stay here and keep fighting endless battles until I figured out another way to escape.

"For a while I hated Ryan for ruining my life by making me have to keep living it." I surprise myself by saying the words out loud to her.

"But you don't feel that way now, do you?" Clare looks so worried that I want to reach into the screen and give her a hug.

"No, I don't. But I'm still not sure how to be strong enough to deal with everything."

"You're one of the strongest people I know. You have to be brave just to get through each day. Lucas and Caleb both think you're a tough kid. They've told me that lots of times."

"Really? That's actually really cool coming from two guys who are older and definitely wiser than I am."

"And I don't see why Benjamin would think of you as weak."

"I just feel like now he sees me as someone with problems, you know? Someone he wants to help. I don't want to be that. I want to be someone he just wants to be with."

"All you can do is talk to him."

"I'm afraid I might have done too much of that already."

"How did he seem?"

"What do you mean?"

"After you told him? Did he seem different with you? Did he run away screaming?" I laugh at her.

"No. Actually, he said he was proud of me. That I could talk to him anytime. I just hope that doesn't mean he wants to be my therapist instead of my friend." Instead of my *boyfriend*.

"Look at us. We talk all the time, but I'm your friend, right? Not your therapist. I know this because you don't pay me anything, and real therapists make a shitload." She grins, and I smile back.

"I guess you're right. I just panicked."

"Well, you wouldn't be the first person to do that. Liking someone makes you nuts sometimes. Most of the time."

"Does Ryan make you nuts?"

"Definitely. He's so cute and nice and funny, but talking to him is like trying to talk to a wall sometimes. It's hard enough to be in a long-distance relationship. It would be nice if he was more open. Like you."

"Don't say that to him. He'd tell me to stop talking to you."

"Seeing as he isn't the boss of who I talk to, that would not be a problem."

"Maybe it will be easier for you next year when he moves to Bainesville."

"I hope so. A year in the same city would be nice. Assuming he gets in. Did you get your acceptance letter yet?"

"No, but it should be soon. They said it would come by the end of March."

"Well, I have my fingers crossed. It would be fun to have both of you here."

"Yeah, then I wouldn't have to bug you online at seven in the morning. I could just come to your house and bug you in person."

"That would be great. We could do breakfast."

"Speaking of which, my mom is downstairs cooking for me. I'd better go. Thanks so much, Clare."

"Anytime. If you see that boyfriend of mine, give him a kiss from me."

"That would scare the shit out of him!" She lights up the screen with a huge smile.

"Make sure you have your phone ready. I want a selfie," she says as her face fades from sight.

I'm laughing as I head down the hall toward the smell of pancakes.

thirteen

"Come on, it's right up here! I can't believe you've never done this before!" Benjamin calls back over his shoulder, his neck twisted around so that he can see me. I want to scream at him to watch where he's going, tell him that I don't want him to get hurt, but I don't want to sound pushy or pathetic, so I just smile and try to get my pedals turning faster so that I can keep up. *I* can believe I've never done this before. This is some distance away from being fun. My thighs are screaming at me to slow down and coast a while. My eyes and mouth are full of sand because Benjamin thinks that biking down a steep *dirt* road is the most wonderful thing anyone has ever done on a sunny Saturday afternoon.

I grind my teeth into a smile, making a lovely crunching sound as the sand works its way into my molars, and I put everything I have into getting closer to him…literally and

111

figuratively. Or is it still literally when you mean emotional closeness? A better question would be, why am I thinking about vocabulary when I'm heading down a ninety-degree slope on a bike that I've never ridden before, which probably has some sort of brake mechanism somewhere, but in this moment I have no idea where that might be. I'm going to kill myself.

Now that's something I never say out loud. Especially if Ryan's around.

And now I'm thinking about Ryan. Meanwhile, Benjamin is almost out of sight. I can hear him whooping and laughing as he whips down the hill. I'm not sure, but it looks like he's taken both feet off the pedals, sticking them out to the side. I'm even less sure of this, but it almost looks like he's got his hands in the air as well. The guy is crazy. Gorgeous, funny, outrageous, *and* crazy!

I still can't believe we're actually here, together. After I basically vomited out all of my personal garbage onto him at the bridge, I was terrified he'd either start avoiding me or decide that he had to join Ryan's team of Jack's bodyguards. But he just kept being Benjamin. Walking home from school with me, eating fries at the Supe, with my mom being so nice to both of us that I almost had to tell her to stop. We even went down to the bridge a few more times and managed to just enjoy the view without any more true confessions to mess up the morning.

And now we're here. He invited me to come on a weekend bike ride, which according to Clare is an actual date. Of course, she only knows what I tell her, so I might have skewed the situation in my favor a bit when I told her about it. But it doesn't matter anyhow because right now all I can do is pray that I don't fall off and ruin whatever this is before we even get it started.

I grip the handles so tightly that my knuckles shine through my skin and my fingers start to cramp up. I'm hunched way down over the handlebars with my head bent up at an uncomfortable angle so I can still see. Every inch of me is uncomfortable, but this is still the best day of my life. It's just me and Benjamin in the sunshine, and any minute now I'm actually going to be close enough to see him.

I hear a rumbling behind me and realize that it's just me, Benjamin, and a car that is coming up really fast. I brace myself as it whips by me. It's actually a half-ton pickup truck, the kind with a muffler that's so loud it sounds like there's a hole in it.

I watch it barrel down the hill toward Benjamin. I really hope he isn't making so much noise himself that he can't hear the really impressive muffler. Truck drivers think they rule the roads around here, which they end up actually doing because the rest of us have no choice but to get out of their way. I try to watch what's happening and keep control of my own bike at the same time. I can just see the truck as it gets so close to Benjamin that it almost looks like it's going to ram into him.

Suddenly the truck slows down. Benjamin turns his head toward the passenger side window, as if he's listening to someone talking to him, and then he goes back to watching the road. The truck seems to hold back for a second, letting Benjamin get ahead. Then suddenly it speeds up, grinding into the gravel, spitting it up in a big swirling mess as it seems to swerve toward the shoulder and then straighten out before taking off down the hill and disappearing into its own cloud of dust.

I'm still moving forward, coughing a little as the dust and dirt find their way into my face. I risk removing one hand from my death grip on the handle and wipe my face so that I can see how close I am to Benjamin.

But I can't see him. There's nothing except the road, stretching for miles until it disappears to wherever the asshole in the white truck decided to go.

Where did he go?

My pounding heart starts skipping beats in panic as I finally come up to the place where the truck slowed down beside Benjamin's bike. It's at a spot where the hill starts to ease back from a steep incline to a gentle slope, and I manage to remember how to apply the brakes and slow myself down. In my hurry, I try to get off my bike before it stops completely, and I end up falling onto the gravel with the front wheel spinning in my face. I push it aside, shoving the bike off me as I stand up.

"Benjamin!" I yell it loud enough to create an echo, but there's no answer. I look around frantically, spinning in circles until I'm dizzy from the motion and my panic. I start to run up and down the shoulder, swiveling my head left and right trying to see in all directions at once.

And then I see him.

There's a steep embankment at the side of the road, pitching down into a rock-filled ditch. Benjamin is lying on the rocks, his bike beside him, twisted and broken. I can't tell from here whether Benjamin is twisted and broken too. My head feels light, as if my brain leaked out my ears, leaving it empty and hollow. I can't find any thoughts as I start trying to scramble my way down the grass and stones to where he's lying. I keep falling, then sliding before struggling to get up again, until I just give up and slide all the way down, ignoring the stones digging into me and tearing my clothes.

"Benjamin!" I call out to him as I hit bottom and then start crawling over to him military style. He doesn't answer. Doesn't even turn his head.

His head. It's covered in blood. He must have hit it on a rock when he fell. I can feel my stomach lurch as I stare at it, trying to figure out where the steady flood of red is coming from.

I move closer and gently put my hands on his cheeks, turning his head carefully to the side. I have to swallow hard when I see the massive cut on the back of his head. The blood is pouring out of him, dripping down onto the ground beneath him like some kind of horrible crimson waterfall. I stare at the stones painted red with his blood and for a second it reminds me of the art project that made him so proud.

Red for life.

Except that this red could mean the opposite! I feel a moment of blind panic, black spots shifting in front of my eyes making it impossible to see what I need to do. I take a deep shuddering breath.

Don't you dare pass out! You need to pull it together. He needs you to stay calm. You have to get the bleeding to stop.

I look around for something to use but obviously there's

nothing here but rocks and dirt. I quickly rip my shirt off over my head and bunch it up so that I can press it on the gash, carefully so I don't fill it full of germs in the process. I dig around in my back pocket with my other hand, hoping that my cell phone didn't fall out on my way down to Benjamin. It's still there so I pull it out to call 9-1-1. Nothing happens. No bars. No reception at the bottom of an embankment at the bottom of a hill at the bottom of nowhere.

I have to get help. I can't do this alone. I need Ryan. He's the town superhero, saver of people's lives. Well, my life anyway.

What would he do? Did he panic when he was saving me the way I'm panicking right now?

I bet he thought to check and see if I was alive.

I try to take Benjamin's pulse, but my hands are shaking so much that I can't feel anything. I bend down and put my ear on his chest instead, listening for his heart. I think I can hear it, but my ears are so filled with the sensation of my own heart's out of control pounding that I can't be sure. I sit up and rest one hand gently on his chest, letting out my own breath when I realize that my hand is moving up and down with his breathing.

Now what?

"Help! Someone help!" I scream it as loud as I can, but it's hopeless. No one is going to hear me from up on the road.

I keep applying pressure and screaming for help until my throat is so hoarse that I can't swallow let alone yell. Enough time has passed that the sun is starting to set, disappearing behind the clouds and making everything seem so much worse that it takes everything in me to stop myself from crying.

I bet Super Ryan didn't cry. Then again, he dragged me out of the water first thing in the morning with the sun coming up instead of going down. Completely different scenario. *Right.*

I take a deep breath and slowly move the blood-soaked shirt away from Benjamin's head to see if the bleeding has stopped. It's hard to tell in the dusky light, but it seems like it might have at least slowed down.

It's now or never. I have to leave him long enough to get up to the road and try to flag someone down while there's still a chance they'll see me.

I put the shirt back on the cut, taking my belt off to secure it tightly enough to maybe make a difference if it starts to bleed again. Guess I should have thought of that sooner.

I push myself back up the embankment, trying to stay on my feet long enough to stop from sliding back down. I get up to the top where my bike is still lying forlornly in the middle of the road.

Great. That means either no one has come by in all of this time or people are in such a big freaking hurry that they just swerved around my bike without wondering what it's doing there.

I stand at the side of the road as moist evening air wraps around me, the heavy darkness creeping in much too fast, weighing me down as I start to pray for a set of headlights to come and save us before it's too late.

fourteen

"Can you please explain to us one more time exactly what you saw the truck do?" The cop is bending toward me, her breath sending a puff of garlic into my face with each word, which is making my stomach lurch uncomfortably until I'm afraid I'm going to puke on her shiny police-issue shoes.

"It passed me going down the hill, going really fast. I thought it was just going to keep moving past Benjamin as well, but it slowed down. It looked like someone inside the truck was talking to him, but I can't be sure because I was too far away. Then it swerved toward the shoulder, toward Benjamin. I think. I'm not sure. Then it was gone, and Benjamin was gone."

I've already said this three times, and my voice is starting to sound like a robotic telemarketer. The cops are looking at me like they think I'm full of shit. Even worse, like somehow they think this is all my fault.

I'm tired and scared. I want to know where Benjamin is and what's happening to him. Everything since the headlights finally appeared has blurred together into some kind of surreal nightmare that I can't seem to wake up from. I just have to keep going over and over the story as if, somehow, it'll magically change into something that makes sense to the people listening.

It doesn't even make sense to me. How could I be watching Benjamin singing and whooping it up one second and then be trying to stop his head from bleeding out the next? How did I end up here in the hospital, wearing a hospital gown, because my shirt is covered in Benjamin's blood, and being questioned by a couple of cops who don't seem to like my answers, even though they're the only ones I've got?

I'm so tired my eyelids feel like they're too heavy for my face. My legs hurt from the millions of scratches I put on them sliding down the embankment. I need these guys to leave me alone so I don't accidentally cry. Boys don't cry in public. It's a rule.

"Hey, Jack!" I turn my head at the sound of Ryan's voice. He comes wheeling across the floor, with his mother beside him.

"Hello, Jack," his mom says to me, reaching over and touching me gently on the cheek. I take a deep breath and nod at her. She turns and looks at the two cops.

"He looks very tired. I think he needs to rest. His mother is on her way. If you need to question him anymore, I would suggest you wait for her to arrive." She folds her arms and gives the cops a look that she probably perfected on badly behaved grade five students in her school. The garlic-breath cop opens her mouth as if to argue, but Ryan's mom just glares at her until finally she shrugs.

"Fine. We'll get back to him later." She gives me a look and then stomps off, obviously pissed that Mrs. Malloy ruined her fun.

"Thanks," I say, rubbing my hands over my face trying to push back the tears before they decide to make an appearance.

"Are you okay?" Ryan asks, coming up beside me and touching my shoulder. I just shake my head at him.

"Nowhere close."

"I'm so sorry this happened to your friend, honey," Ryan's mom says, wrapping her arm around me and giving me a sideways hug. "Your mom just managed to get away from work and is on her way. You'll feel better once she's here."

I'm so glad Mrs. Malloy called the cops off me that I just want to curl up in a little ball and go to sleep for long enough to forget everything that happened, and Benjamin is all better by the time I wake up. It will all become one of those bad dreams that you know you had but can't fully remember. Just the sensation that something was wrong in the dark but is okay now that your eyes are open.

I don't know what happened. I saw the truck slow down and then speed up, and then Benjamin was just gone. I don't know if the truck hit him or just startled him. I don't know if it was an accident or deliberate.

And if it was deliberate...I really don't want to think about what that means.

"Jack?" Ryan squeezes my shoulder, startling me.

"What?"

"Mom asked you if you'd like something to eat or drink." His eyes are worried, but it doesn't bother me today. I'm worried about me too. I take a deep enough breath that I almost choke on it. I clear my throat, shaking my head at the same time.

"No thanks. I'm good," I tell her. *That's not true. I'm not good at all. Benjamin is lying somewhere in this hospital with his head split open, and I don't know why.*

"Well, let me know if you change your mind. I'm going to go over and see what I can find out about your friend." She walks away, and Ryan shakes his head in a quick little movement as if he's trying to dislodge a fly or something.

"Déjà vu all over again," he says.

"What?"

"I just had a total flashback to the day you…you know…"

"Sent both of us to the hospital?"

"Yeah, I guess that's one way to put it. I remembered my mom saying pretty much those exact words when we were here to have my shoulder checked. I was scared shitless."

"About your shoulder being hurt?"

"That too, but I meant I was scared about you. Seeing you. My parents figured I'd want to know how you were and that I would want to go and see you. Which I didn't. I was terrified of talking to you. I had no idea how to speak to someone who just…"

"Tried to float away down the river on a one-way cruise," I finish for him, too tired to be polite. He looks at me with a startled expression and then flashes a quick grin.

"Yeah, *that*. Everyone figured we were friends, but I didn't even know you. I didn't know how to talk to you."

"Yeah, that was pretty obvious."

Ryan smiles ruefully. "Benjamin *is* your friend, so you must be really worried. Such a shitty accident to have happened to him."

"I hope it was."

He looks at me, eyebrows pushed together in confusion. "What do you mean?"

"I mean, what if it wasn't an accident? I've been sitting here thinking about it. What if those assholes decided to teach the gay guy a lesson? Like gay bashing. Get him when he's away from school and his mom's not around." Saying it out loud is even worse than thinking about it. Is it possible? Could anyone be so filled with hate that they'd actually risk someone else's life to make some warped point?

Which is such a naïve question. And I do know the answer. I live in the real world. I can read. This crap has gone on forever. I know that there are likely still more places in this world that wouldn't accept me for who I am than places that would. I know that there are still countries where there are laws against homosexuality—with punishments that even include death in some places. As if being gay is the same as being a serial killer.

How can it be against the law to fall in love?

"I never even thought of that. That would be seriously warped. I hope that isn't true. But…" Ryan's voice trails away into thought and he closes his eyes for a second.

"But it's possible or more likely *probable* that someone was trying to hurt him, or at the very least scare him." I spit the words out of my mouth, but I can't get rid of the disgusting taste they leave behind.

"Yeah, I think it probably is. And I know someone who might know something about this." Ryan opens his eyes as his voice gets angrier with each word.

"Don't go off and start yelling at Cody. I don't think he'd do something like this."

"Me either, but that doesn't mean he wouldn't know something about it. He hangs out with a lot of supreme assholes. Some of the guys who have been total shits to Benjamin ever since he told everyone about rainbows. And to you since forever. I'm at least going to talk to him."

"Okay. Just don't get into another giant fight with the guy over me."

"It's not really about you this time though. Benjamin is a nice guy. No one should be hassling him, whether they actually tried to hurt him or not. This shit has to stop. I don't care if this is a small town, it doesn't mean we have to be Neanderthals, bashing each other over the head with clubs."

I get this crazy mental image of Ryan wheeling around chasing Cody with a club. For some reason that makes me laugh, a sound that surprises both of us so much that Ryan laughs too.

"I guess I got a bit carried away," he says.

"Maybe, but you're right. Benjamin keeps saying that things will never change if no one tries. But how do you try in a place where all of the assholes are bigger than us?"

"I guess we have to use our big mouths instead. Or find some big clubs."

"I don't think any size clubs would work on some of those guys. Their heads are so thick the club would just bounce off." Ryan starts to laugh but stops quickly as his mother walks over to us with a serious look on her face. My heart does a quick lurch in my chest and my hands start to sweat.

"He's still unconscious. That's all they could tell me. I'm sorry, sweetheart."

I usually love the way she calls me honey and sweetheart, but today it makes me feel like she's feeling sorry for me, over-compensating because she thinks that things are really bad with Benjamin but doesn't want to say anything.

"Mom, I'm going to just sit with him until his mom gets here, which should be soon, right? I'll just meet you at the car," Ryan says to her. She looks at me and then nods. She leans over and gives me a quick kiss on the cheek and then runs her hand over Ryan's hair before heading off.

Ryan looks at me, just waiting. I don't know what for.

"It's okay to be scared," he says.

"That's good, because I am. I don't know what to do. I mean, it's not like we're actually…anything to each other. It's not like they're going to tell me anything or let me in to see him. We had one pseudo date, and it turned into this." I wave one hand at the waiting room full of sick and sad people. A little girl in pajamas waves back with a sweet smile and I suddenly feel a lump in my throat.

"You're friends. They let me see you, and we weren't even that."

"Yeah, but you were the big savior of the year."

"I think that title just passed on to you."

What is he talking about? "What?"

"You saved him. When we first got here and asked where you were, the nurse said 'Oh, you mean the boy who saved that other boy's life.'"

"I only did what I had to do."

"Maybe, but the point is that you got down to where he was and stopped the bleeding. She told us you got back up to the road and managed to flag down a truck. And you saved him. That makes you a hero. Like me." He points at himself with both thumbs, grinning a little. I give him a small one back, shaking my head at the same time. *Am I Benjamin's hero?*

"It wasn't *that* big a deal."

"Yeah, well that's what I kept saying after the day at the bridge too. But it is a big deal. And his parents will likely let you see him once the doctors okay it, because they'll want to thank you. It's the first thing your mother did with me."

"But would he want to see me? If this was you and Clare back at the beginning, would you be the person she would have wanted to see?"

"I don't know. You'd have to ask her. I think I'd want to see her if I was the one in that bed. Anyway, here comes your mother, so I guess I'd better fly. I'll call you later." He wheels away, stopping briefly to talk to my mom. She's still in her waitress uniform, and I can see a brown stain on her skirt where it looks like some of the cook's disgusting excuse for gravy must have landed.

"Jack. Are you all right?" she asks as she sits down beside me. A whiff of grease comes from her apron. Definitely gravy—three parts bacon fat and one part dishwater.

"I wasn't hurt. I was the witness. This is just because my shirt got wrecked." I pull at the shoulder of the hospital gown.

"I'm not talking about that. Look at your legs!"

We both look down to the scratched up, dirty mess. I can see tiny stones embedded in some of the deeper scratches. It looks gross but it's nothing compared to Benjamin's head.

"They don't really hurt. I just slid a bit when I was trying to get down to him. They told me he's still unconscious." My voice hitches.

"They told *me* you saved him." She touches me on the tip of my nose. She looks proud of me.

"Ryan said that too. I didn't have a choice. He was bleeding and I had to stop it. Then I obviously had to get help."

"Well, I think you were brave and level-headed to get to him, stop the bleeding, and manage to get help. Ryan's mother told me the staff here believes he would have actually bled to death if you hadn't done what you did."

I shrug my shoulders. It's nice that people think I'm a hero, but I don't want to talk about this anymore. Benjamin is still unconscious, and Ryan has gone off to see if he can find out if this was an accident or something so much worse that I can't stand thinking about it.

"If Benjamin is still unconscious, there probably isn't much you can do here right now. I think we should go home and get you cleaned up. Unless you want to wait here and have a doctor look at those legs."

"No! No doctors. I'm fine. We can go home, I guess."

She stands up and reaches her hand out to me. I don't really need help getting up, but I take it anyway. She keeps hold of me all the way out to the car. She doesn't ask me anything else about Benjamin. She doesn't ask me anything at all.

fifteen

Ryan was right about Benjamin's parents. Mrs. Lee hugged and kissed me, thanking me over and over again. She told me I could be in his room whenever I wanted and cleared it with the nursing staff so that no one would hassle me when I showed up. She even said that Benjamin talks about me a lot and that he's fond of me. That's the word she used. *Fond.* Not exactly the word I'd be looking for, but I suppose it's better than nothing.

I come here every day after school and just sit. This is day five, and he's still just lying there. There's swelling in his brain because of the force of the impact when he flew down the embankment. His head must have hit first. He also has a fractured hip and some swelling along his spinal cord.

This room looks exactly like the one I ended up in last year and it reminds me of the first conversation I had with Ryan as if it were yesterday.

✱ ✱ ✱

I was more tired than I could ever remember feeling. Which is why I was doubly pissed when I heard my mother talking to the guy who saved me. The great rescuer of people who would rather be left alone.

I listened to her thanking him for being a hero and to him sounding all humble. When my mother asked him what happened, my heart lurched a little, and I turned toward him. I figured he was revving up to tell her my secret so that my worst nightmare could continue.

Except he didn't. He told my mother that I had fallen off the bridge and he'd gone in after me. That was it. End of story.

He lied for me. I couldn't understand why the hell he would do that.

Then, making things more awkward, my mother suddenly got up and left us alone.

"Why?" My voice came out into the room without my permission.

"What?" He seemed startled that I could talk.

"Why?" I repeated.

"It looked like you were drowning. I couldn't just sit and watch."

"No. Not that. Why did you say I *fell?*"

"I…didn't know what to say, I guess. I wasn't sure what really happened."

"You saw me?" I looked up at the ceiling, embarrassed that he'd probably seen me dancing in my mother's skirt. The implications of someone catching me like that were so devastating, I couldn't bear to think about it.

"Yeah."

"Did anyone else see?" My voice trembled a bit, and I bit down on my lip to force some self-control.

"No. Just me. I took your…um…stuff off and hid it."

"Why?"

"I don't know. I thought you might not want anyone to see it or something. Just a guess."

"Okay." I closed my eyes. I figured he was playing up the superhero crap for all it was worth, talking to everyone who'd listen: my mom, the doctors, his friends. Not to mention the cops.

My eyes flew open. "What will you tell the cops?"

"I guess that depends on what they ask me."

"I don't want anyone to know. Not yet, anyway. Just keep saying I fell off the bridge. An accident. Whatever. Just for now. *Please?*" The last thing I wanted was to ask him for anything, but the truth would create endless questions that I didn't have any answers to.

"Yeah, it's cool. I'll just say I saw you in the water. That's mostly true." He looked like he was scared of me. It was almost funny seeing as I was lying there, helpless.

Ryan did cover for me, but it didn't help much. The adults in my life took about three seconds to realize that any version of me accidentally ending up in the water at five thirty in the morning was likely some distance from the truth.

* * *

Looking back now, I appreciate the guts it took for Ryan to come and see me. I didn't make it easy for him. I was too twisted up inside to worry about what he was feeling.

And now I'm still twisted up, but this time it's because I'm worrying about Benjamin. It's hurting my heart to just sit here waiting for him to wake up. I want to *do* something, but I don't know what!

He *is* going to wake up. I have to believe that or I'm pretty sure my heart will go from just hurting to completely disintegrating. The doctors are calling it a coma now. I don't know what the difference is between being unconscious and being in a coma, except that the second one sounds a lot more dramatic. I don't want to ask or look it up because I don't really want to know. It doesn't matter what you label it, he's sleeping, and eventually he's going to wake up. He has to.

He wouldn't like the pale green hospital gown they stuck him in. Benjamin likes bright colors, with crazy combinations that would shock your average fashion guru and look terrible on anyone but him. He also won't be too happy when he sees his hair. There's a big section at the back that they had to shave to clean the cut and see the damage. You can't see it from where I'm sitting though. The rest of his hair is spread across his pillow, all fanned out like some kind of dark brown halo. His mom has been brushing it for him every day. My throat aches each time I watch her carefully taking small sections of hair and working the brush through them until every strand shimmers, making his beautiful brown hair the brightest thing in the room.

He's so still, silent, and ghost-like under the white blanket, which is tucked cleanly into the sides of the white mattress on the white metal bed. Why is everything in a hospital so white? Do they think it makes it feel cleaner or something? Sterility denoted by a complete lack of color?

I know some people see black as the color of death, but I think it's white. My mother has this picture of her version of heaven on the wall at home. White, billowy clouds surround several angels who are all dressed in white robes with white wings. Even their faces are white, because apparently when you go to Heaven you get a makeover so you can fit in.

I think I'd rather be in my mom's idea of hell. At least there's some color down there, lots of red anyway. According to Benjamin, it's the color of life. And hell would be warmer than this place that seems to have the air conditioning on high twenty-four seven. It's springtime outside and winter in here.

I walk over to the bed and stand looking down at Benjamin. My throat starts to swell up again, and I have to swallow several times to get it to stop. I can't be standing here choking on tears when his mom comes back in. She's been so incredible—talking to him as if he's listening, reading, and playing music. Making plans for when he's better.

All I do is stare. I don't trust my voice, and besides, I can't think of anything intelligent to say. It feels like we're stuck inside some kind of strange fairy tale and Benjamin is waiting for true love's kiss to wake him up.

Now I'm staring at his mouth.

"Hey." Ryan's voice startles me, and I jump a little.

"Hi," I say to him, keeping my voice hushed as if I'm trying not to wake Benjamin up when the exact opposite is true.

"No change?"

"Not that I can see. They're always coming in and checking things, but no one ever says anything. His mom is due back soon, so she might know more." Ryan nods, looking over at the bed and then taking a three-sixty glance at the rest of the room.

"Man, I still remember coming in to talk to you that day. I so didn't want to be there." He smiles a little.

"Yeah, well, news flash. I didn't want you there. I wanted you to go straight to hell."

"That was fairly obvious at the time. It was probably the most awkward, uncomfortable conversation of my life."

"We've had a few of those, I think."

He looks at me for a second as if he doesn't know what I'm talking about. Then he sighs and nods. "I know," he says. "I'm awkward and uncomfortable around you a lot. It makes me feel stupid, but I don't know how to stop."

"It's better than it used to be. It used to suck. I didn't know if you were my friend or my babysitter." I'm still speaking quietly, glancing over at the bed every time I say anything.

"That's fair. I don't always know either. I guess I've always been...scared."

"Of me? Because I'm gay?"

"No. Not that. Not at all! Just...of how sad you were. I thought if I said or did anything wrong that I could push you back."

"Back into the water?"

"The water or something else." He takes a deep breath and looks me straight in the eyes. "I didn't know how to deal with thinking that you wanted to die and worrying that you might want to try it again." He finally just puts it out there into the room where we both can see it hanging, waiting for a reaction.

My only reaction is an overwhelming sense of relief.

"I can understand that. It would make it hard to relax around me." I try a smile, and he grins back a little.

"It's not like that so much now though. You seem...different. Not so sad. Even now, when you're so worried about Benjamin, I don't feel that...panic thing around you that I used to." He shrugs uncomfortably. He's doing some Clare-style talking here and is obviously miles out of anything resembling his comfort zone. I feel a bit sorry for him, but I'm glad he's doing it.

"I am different. And you don't have to panic around me anymore. So, does this mean you're done with the whole Super Ryan thing?"

"Super Ryan? You call me that too? I thought that was Cody's obnoxious nickname for me."

"I won't call you that anymore. You're not so super anyway."

"Nope. I'll pass that one over to you. Super Jack."

"Jackson."

We both turn toward the bed. My heart starts beating so hard that it sounds like a helicopter just flew into the room as I look into Benjamin's open eyes.

"Super Jack*son*," he says softly, as his lips curve ever so slightly into a smile.

sixteen

"I guess no one told you that I woke up earlier today. I don't remember it very well because the whole world was…*is* pretty groggy. I didn't know where I was or why my head hurt. I'm still not very clear on the details." Benjamin smiles weakly. After the shock of hearing his voice, Ryan headed out to get a nurse who wasn't nearly as surprised as we were. Once we realized we hadn't just witnessed a miracle, Ryan not so subtly realized he had somewhere else to be and disappeared.

"So, you were lying there listening just now or did we wake you up?"

"A little of each. I'm glad you and Ryan figured a few things out."

"Yeah, well I guess it's been a long time coming, but I'm sorry that we decided to do that in your hospital room. Not exactly entertaining for you."

He smiles, closing his eyes briefly as if it's too much effort to keep them open.

"Are you getting tired? Do you want me to leave?"

"Yes and no," he says, eyes still shut.

"Yes you're tired but no you don't want me to leave?" I say hopefully.

"Right and right. Can you tell me what happened? I'm just going to listen with my eyes closed. All this white shit is giving me a headache. If I pass out, don't be offended."

I knew he'd hate the "color scheme" in this room! I should go and get his rainbow project from the art room and tack it to the wall opposite his bed. Brighten up the place. Although, it's so heavy that it would probably fall down and sprinkle colored stones all over the floor, which would piss off the staff.

"Okay. So, you just want me to tell you everything I remember? You don't have any questions to start?"

"I don't even remember enough to know what to ask." He rubs his forehead slightly as if it hurts.

I'm not so sure talking about this right now is a good idea. I feel like I should ask someone's permission or something like that. But I don't want to treat him like a baby either. He asked me to do it. I don't see where I have a choice. I reach back into my memory and take a deep breath.

"Well, we were going down the hill. I was way behind you because I suck at bike riding, which I didn't tell you when you asked me to come because I didn't want you to find someone else to go with." He grins slightly, and I clear my throat before continuing. "So, I was pushing to keep up, and you were already halfway down, going a hundred miles an hour and singing or yelling or something loud. I couldn't really tell from where I was. Then this big-ass truck comes out of nowhere and whips by me heading down to where you are." His brow furrows, like he's trying to think about my words. He rubs his forehead again. He really looks like he's in some kind of pain.

"Are you okay? Does your head hurt? Should I get the nurse?" I interrupt myself to ask.

"No. It's all right. Keep going. I'm just trying to follow what you're saying." His voice is so weak it makes my stomach do a panic flop, but I keep talking. The sooner I get this over with, the better.

"It slowed down when it got close. You were looking at the passenger side window, so I thought maybe someone said something to you. Then the truck seemed to stop for a second before it suddenly took off. It looked like it swerved toward the shoulder and then headed away so fast that it disappeared. It only took a few seconds for it all to happen, and I was down to your spot right after, but you were gone. Just gone." The panic flop comes back and turns into a full-on nightmare as I remember that next horrible moment.

"Then I saw you. You'd fallen down the embankment and hurt yourself. I tried to stop the bleeding and then flagged down some help." I try to keep my tone calm and matter-of-fact so that my voice doesn't tell him how terrifying it really was.

"Super Jackson," he whispers, opening his eyes for a second.

"I don't know about that. But at least you're here and you're okay." *I hope.*

He nods and then winces.

"I keep forgetting that moving makes me dizzy."

"Maybe you should sleep now."

"Okay. Can you stay for a bit?"

"Sure." *Does forever count as a bit?*

I sit on the chair beside his bed and watch him. He looks worried, as if my words upset him. I wish I could reach over and touch his face, stroking away the lines that I think I just put there. But I can't. All I can do is to keep watching until his muscles start to relax and his breathing becomes rhythmic enough that I can tell he's fallen asleep. I reach over and touch the back of his hand gently and tiptoe out of the room.

"Hi, Jack." Mrs. Lee is walking toward me, a bag in one hand and what looks like Benjamin's cell phone in the other.

"Hi, Mrs. Lee. I think he's sleeping." She nods.

"That's good. He's still very tired. I brought him a few things that I'm hoping will keep him relaxed. Some books to read to him and his phone. It has all of his music." She smiles but it doesn't reach her eyes. They look tired and full of worry.

"He'll be happy to have the music. I think he'd like a can of paint, too. His room is pretty white."

"That would be a great idea if we could. It might encourage him to keep his eyes open more now that he's awake. The doctor says to be patient though. The light probably bothers him."

"That makes sense." *Does it though? Does any of this make sense?*

"He has a long road ahead of him, Jack. The doctors said it's going to take patience and support. His hip will take a lot of recovery time, and they still don't know about his back. His head injury is significant and might cause some memory loss or trouble with other things."

"Other things?"

"Well, sometimes this kind of injury can cause fine motor difficulty. For example, make it difficult to draw. That kind of thing."

"He's kind of a terrible artist anyway," I say without thinking. Mrs. Lee lets out a startled laugh as I clamp my hand over my mouth. "Shit! I mean, shoot. I shouldn't have said that."

"That's okay. It's true. He loves art though, and he's always telling me how he wishes he could be as talented as you are."

"Really? I'm always wishing I could be more like him."

"He is quite a kid." Her voice hitches a bit on the last word, and she sniffs as she starts digging in her purse for a Kleenex, as if it's the most important thing in the world at this exact moment.

"He's really strong. I'm sure he'll be fine." *I'm sure he'll be fine.* That's comforting coming from a medical genius like myself.

"I know. He's my champion. I just wish I could understand what happened. He's a much better athlete than he is an artist, and he's never fallen like this before." She looks at me in the same way the cops did. Like she's looking for answers that for some reason I have hidden away from everyone.

"I wish I understood it too. I just didn't see. I'm sorry." I have both hands out toward her, palms up as if I'm trying to hand her my apology.

"Oh, honey. You have nothing to be sorry for! If you hadn't been there…well, I can't even let myself think about it." She reaches over and pulls me into a quick hug, the bag of books bumping gently against my back. It should feel a little weird being hugged by my VP, but here in this hospital, away from school, she's just Benjamin's mom, and it feels okay. I hug her back and then we both step away.

"I'm going to go in, so he isn't alone when he wakes up. Are you heading home?" she asks.

"Yeah, Mom is expecting me for supper. She wanted me to tell you she's praying for Benjamin and that she lit a candle for him in church on Sunday." I wasn't sure if I was going to tell her that or not. I don't know if people appreciate being prayed for when their religion is different from yours. My mom has this idea that everyone sees the world the same way she does, and that her particular brand of religious beliefs provides some kind of comfort to people who likely see it as just the opposite. Mrs. Lee is Jewish and Mr. Lee is Buddhist. My mom is Catholic. I stay away from anything resembling a church.

"Tell her thank you. It means a lot to me that she would do that." She smiles gently, looking honestly pleased as she heads into Benjamin's room.

I watch her go in and sit by his bed, gently taking his hand in hers, leaning forward as she puts her forehead against his and just stays there, face to face. I'm not sure, but it seems like she's whispering to him.

It looks a bit like a prayer.

seventeen

"I've been checking around like you asked me to," Cody says, sounding as defensive as I've ever heard him. He's pacing around Ryan's room like an animal caught in a trap. He's avoiding eye contact, looking down at his own feet as they stomp their way across the floor for the twentieth time.

"Would you please stand still for one second? You're making me dizzy." Ryan does a quick shift to avoid Cody walking straight into his wheelchair. I'm sitting on the bed, out of potential harm's way, just watching and listening. I'm too tired to say anything. I'll let Ryan do the talking.

"Fine!" Cody shouts and sits down on Ryan's chair, propping both feet up on his desk. His shoes look like he wore them to muck out a pig barn, and they smell even worse. Ryan just shakes his head, looking disgusted.

"Nice, Cody. Make yourself at home."

"Thanks. I will." Cody shifts his feet, crossing his ankles so that dirt rains down on everything sitting on the desk. Ryan leans forward to rescue some pages of the graphic novel we were working on before the world fell apart and then glowers at Cody.

"Shit, Cody. What the hell is your problem? You're being a total jerk."

"My problem? You want to know what my problem is? My problem is that you sent me out looking to see if someone hurt your friend's little buddy. And I've had to sneak around trying to find things out that I don't even want to know. It's bad enough that people know I'm friends with you, and you're friends with him." He points at me. "It's already screwed royally with my rep. And now I'm asking questions that I shouldn't be asking, and people are starting to talk about me. You have no idea what I'm going through."

We both stare at him in amazement. Seriously, does he ever actually listen to himself? Does he see who he's sitting here with?

"You are kidding, right?" Ryan asks incredulously. Cody looks royally pissed.

"No, I'm not. And I know what you're thinking. But you guys are used to it. People have always stared at you or talked behind your back. It's just part of your deal. But this is not my deal."

"No, you're usually doing the staring and the talking."

Cody glowers at Ryan for several seconds. Then he sighs slightly in a way that almost sounds sad.

"It's what I do. And sometimes I kick ass when I need to. Like I did for you two wuss babies that day at the dumpsters."

"Wuss babies. Very nice." Ryan rolls his eyes.

"Whatever. Those guys had it coming. There was nothing cool about those idiots coming after you. I don't mind a fair fight. And I never saw the big deal with a few carefully chosen insults now and then, just to keep life interesting."

"Except when the insults are thrown at you," Ryan says, pointing at Cody with both index fingers.

"Even then it's no big deal if I'm giving it back. I don't like this talking behind my back crap that's going on, but I can't make it stop."

"I don't even know why we're having a conversation about what you do or don't like. You're supposed to be telling us what you know about Benjamin." Ryan's voice rises in frustration as Cody slides his feet off the desk, bringing them down to the floor with a loud thump and sending up a cloud of pig-shit dust. He leans forward, putting both hands on his knees, and just stares at the desktop.

"What I know about Benjamin is that no one had the right to go after him like that. Words are one thing. Knocking him into the ditch is something else," Cody says, gripping his knees so hard that he must be hurting himself.

"Knocking him into the ditch? As in deliberately? Did someone tell you that's what happened?" I jump off the bed and stand beside him. He looks up at me. There's something in his eyes that I've never seen there before.

"Not directly. But I listened. Asked a few questions. I

know who was in the truck. I know they saw him there and decided to give him a hard time. I don't know if they knocked him down on purpose, but from what I heard, they were trying to scare him, and they knew he was down and just left him there."

"Who was it?" I grind the question out through gritted teeth. My body is vibrating with an anger so intense, I might burst into flames.

Cody just shakes his head.

"Cody, you have to tell. These assholes can't get away with this. Even you can see that, can't you?" Ryan comes up beside me and puts one hand on my arm. I must be vibrating so much that he can see it.

"Even I can see that? Yes, Ryan, even stupid Cody McNeely can see that knocking some poor kid off his bike into the ditch and driving away like a frigging coward is wrong. I just…can't believe it."

"What do you mean?" Ryan asks.

"I mean what I said. I can't believe that they would take it this far. I mean, I hear the talk and even the threats all the time, but no one goes through with any of it. It's just talk. It doesn't really hurt anyone." I wonder if he really thinks that's true. If he can actually be that oblivious. I want to ask, but I don't dare distract him. I have to know who did this, so I just keep my mouth shut and let Cody keep talking. "This is different. Whether they actually tried to hit him or not, they knew it was dangerous to be screwing around with a truck and a bike like that. They just didn't care. They put that kid in the hospital."

"Benjamin," I say quietly.

"What?" Cody looks up at me.

"His name is Benjamin. And he's smart and nice and funny. He's good at sports, just like you are. He's a person just like you are, only better. And your friends just treated him like garbage."

"They aren't my friends. Far from it. And in spite of what you may think, I'm not okay with this shit. I don't want this to be some town you hear about on the news because people get hurt by local assholes."

"So, do something about it. Report what you know. Help it not happen to someone else." Ryan's voice sounds both frustrated and tired now, and I know how he feels.

Cody shifts his eyes to Ryan. "I don't really *know* anything. I mean, I know, but I don't. I just heard things. No one told me directly. If I snitch and can't back it up, I've just screwed myself for all eternity, and it won't make any difference."

"It doesn't matter if you have proof. That's the cops' job. If you have any information, you need to tell them. Get off your self-pity train and do the right thing for a change." I'm practically growling and they both look at me in surprise.

"Self-pity train?" Cody starts to grin. Ryan takes one look at him and laughs, which makes me start smiling even though nothing about this is remotely funny.

"It's not funny," Ryan says, even though he's the one laughing.

"It is a little. Jackie baby getting all tough and scary." Cody grins at me full-on for a second and then sobers up. "I am

147

sorry and pissed that your friend got hurt. And I will tell what I heard, and ruin my life, if you really think it will make things better. But only to the cops. Not you." He shoots me an expression worthy of any of the martyrs my mother likes to pray to.

"I want to know."

"You'll know when everyone knows, and when the cops are on it. I don't want you going off and getting all fierce and then getting the shit kicked out of you. I don't have the energy to rescue you again."

"He's right, Jack. Let the cops deal with it," Ryan says quietly.

I take a deep breath. I know they're right, but I still want to know now. I want to look those assholes in the eyes and tell them I know who and what they are.

But getting the shit kicked out of me won't help Benjamin, so I concede. "Okay. We'll do it your way."

"I don't think it's exactly my way, but I'll do it—later," Cody says. Ryan stares at him, eyebrows raised, head shaking slowly, back and forth.

"Now? You want me to go right now?" Cody asks, sounding wounded. "You don't trust me to go later?"

"Not one little bit. If I had my license, I'd drive you there myself just to make sure," Ryan says, wheeling toward the door. "And don't let the door hit your ass on the way out." He smiles as Cody stands up and marches to the door, looking like he's headed for his last supper on death row.

"Cody?"

He turns back at the sound of my voice. "What?"

"Thank you. You're doing the right thing."

"Yeah, yeah. Whatever. Every time I get involved with you, someone makes me do the right thing. It sucks." He scowls at Ryan and walks out of the room, leaving Ryan and me alone.

"Do you think he'll actually do it? Rat out someone he knows?" I ask.

"I think he will. I think this whole thing really shocked him. Cody acts like a jerk, but he likes to save people more than he likes to hurt them. Physically anyway."

"Do you believe that he actually doesn't understand how much words can hurt someone?" There have been times I would have preferred having someone just hit me and get it over with instead of continually going at me with cruel little comments that get inside and try to break me apart.

"It's possible. He's always lived in his own little Cody box, where he sits and looks at the world in his own little Cody way. At least until now. He actually seems really shook up by this. And it takes a lot to shake him."

"This *is* a lot. It's been two weeks and Benjamin is still lying in the hospital."

"How's he doing?"

"His mom said that the big issue is the swelling on his spine. They have to wait for it to go down more so they can see if there's any permanent damage. He's got feeling and movement in his feet and legs, so that's good. He'll likely be in a wheelchair until his fractured hip heals when he does get out."

"We can be chair buddies. They finally renovated the guys'

can on the main floor at school, so he won't even have to use the staff room."

"You graduate in like, two months!"

"Yup. The school board is known for its great speed. Anyway, I guess it'll help the next guy who comes along. And for now, it'll help Benjamin."

"I don't know if he's even coming back to school this year. The head injury has given him some memory problems. Short-term, they called it. He forgets things you just said to him and you have to repeat it all." I've had to give him the details of his "accident" at least three times now. I finally wrote it all down and emailed it to him so he could read it. Then I found out he's having trouble reading too. He can't remember what he just read when he finishes a page, which is scary because this is a guy who usually reads three books a week and can quote from each one whenever he feels like it.

What if his head never comes back to normal? If he can't read or remember anything, how will he finish school and go to college and get a job?

When I find out who did this…

"Jack?"

"What?"

"I asked you if he's going to be able to rehab here."

"Sorry. I didn't hear you. I was…thinking. What do you mean, *rehab* here?"

"Well, the hospital here has physio and occupational thera-pists, but only a couple of each, so there's always a waiting list. The equipment here is pretty minimal too. After my surgeries,

I've always stayed in the city for a few weeks for the intense part of my rehab. They have a good center there and since it's Benjamin's hometown, I thought he might end up there for a while...*and* I can see from your face that you hadn't thought of that. Sorry, I should have kept my mouth shut."

"No, no. That's okay. You're right. I never thought he'd have to go away. But obviously he needs the best, so if that's what it takes...I can just talk to him the way you do with Clare." If he wants to, that is.

"The way *you* do with Clare, you mean. I'm pretty sure you talk to her more than I do." He laughs.

"Well, she's really helpful and probably the nicest person I know next to Benjamin."

"Thanks."

"You come third. Or maybe fourth." He smacks me with his pillow, making me laugh.

"Benjamin *is* nicer than me, and he seems like a really strong guy. He'll get through this. And if Cody does what he said he would do, the assholes who did this will get caught and have to pay somehow."

"If they can prove it was deliberate."

"I don't know how they can prove it, but obviously they did something wrong. Benjamin didn't throw himself down the embankment and try to kill himself on purpose." I look at him and he closes his eyes, scrunching up his face. "Shit, Jack. I didn't mean..."

"Hey, we talked about this, right? No more Super Ryan. We can't pretend it didn't happen, but it doesn't mean you have to watch every word you say to me. I don't want you to. I don't even notice until you panic and think you've said something that will upset me or trigger me or something. It's time for you to stop. Okay? I'm good. I'm not going anywhere."

"Okay. I know. I get it. Seriously."

"Good because I *seriously* don't need a babysitter anymore." He grins and nods. "Anyway, I have to get over to the hospital. Thanks for helping with Cody. I guess now we just have to wait and see what happens next."

"You know that's true, right? That you can't go off and try to confront the guys when you learn their names." His face turns serious.

"I really, really want to go and kick their stupid faces in."

"But you really, really can't. Let the cops do what they do. You just focus on helping Benjamin. He's going to need all the friends he can get to see him through this."

"He'll have all of his old friends if he goes back home." I can hear the sulky kid tone in my own voice.

"Doesn't mean he won't need you too. Clare has lots of friends where she lives. She still seems to like me for some reason."

"She does. I've always wondered about that."

"It's my stunning good looks and endless charm." He smiles, showing lots of teeth like a baboon trying to impress gawkers at the zoo.

"Oh, well, that explains it then. I think I'll go before I actually puke." I smile back and leave his room, ducking as he throws his pillow at me on my way out.

eighteen

I walk down the hall at school, feeling as if all the color has been leeched out of the world around me and I'm Dorothy stuck in black and white looking for a rainbow to pass over. The only person I know who could make one of those appear out of thin air is lying in a hospital bed instead of walking down the hall toward me with a big smile on his face.

The last time I felt this alone was my first day back at school after Ryan's big rescue. I remember walking down this same hallway with everyone staring, whispering, even pointing…just in case someone didn't know who all the staring and whispering was about. The rumors started down on the ground, getting hotter and hotter as they rose up and swirled around me like Dorothy's tornado, except that this one wasn't going to get me a pair of ruby slippers or a yellow brick road to follow.

I knew I should have stayed home instead of listening to

my mother and forcing myself back to school so that the torture could start all over again. I could have done my courses online. I figured that if I could survive until graduation, I could get the hell out of this town and never come back.

"Jack?"

Startled, I realize that someone is talking directly to me. I shake my head a little to get out of the memory and bring myself forward about ten months.

Ten months. I can't believe it's been less than a year.

"Yeah?" It's Sarah Edey and her mini-gang. I glance around. No one else is paying any attention. No stares or whispers or fingers pointing that I can see.

"I—*we* were just wondering how Benjamin is doing. We heard a rumor that he's moving away or something. Is he okay?" She looks concerned and even touches me gently on the shoulder for a second.

"He's getting better. Slowly. He isn't moving away though. He's just going to a rehab center for a while. He'll be back." I say it forcefully so that everyone will believe it, including me. The truth is that I'm afraid he won't be back. Benjamin's parents might decide that Thompson Mills isn't worth living in, and I'll never see him in person again. And I'd have to try to have an online relationship with someone who'd be surrounded by people he's known his whole life. I'll be even farther away next year because I got my acceptance to Bainesville U, which was exciting for about thirty seconds, until I realized that it probably puts me a county away from Benjamin next year, whether he moves or not. I'm pretty sure he would have applied to much better schools than BU. I never even asked him about it, and now I'm afraid to. Ryan got in too, but for him it's a win-win. He gets away from Thompson Mills *and* he gets to be with Clare. Lucky.

"Well, can you tell him that we're thinking about him? And that we think what happened was just horrible. Everyone does, you know."

"I'll tell him."

"He's a really nice guy," she says. "You two make a cute couple." She takes off before I can say anything.

I stand there, watching her go. She didn't sound like she was making fun of me. It sounded like she meant it. This is too weird.

I turn back to my locker and grab my books for class. As I close the door and lock it, I suddenly feel someone standing right behind me.

"You're going to wish you hadn't said anything."

I stand facing my locker for a second. I know that voice.

Shawn Johanssen. The owner of a white truck. The name that Cody heard but didn't want to tell me. The one that everyone at school is spreading rumors…no, spreading the *truth* about.

One of the assholes who pinned me against a dumpster last year.

The one who hurt Benjamin.

I turn around slowly. "Get out of my face, asshole," I say to him, keeping my voice low and controlled.

"What are you going to do about it? I don't see anyone

here." I look past him. He's right. Class has already started, and the hall is deserted.

"So, what's the plan? You're going to kick my ass right here in the hall? Add that to the list of things the cops can get you on?"

He grabs my shirt and shoves me back against my locker. "The cops aren't getting me on shit. I was just driving my truck like I do every day. It's not my fault some fag can't keep his balance." His breath stinks of cigarette smoke. Good, he deserves to die young.

"Right. That's what happened. He just randomly fell off his bike at the exact moment you swerved toward him." He tightens his grip and shoves me so hard I feel like I'm going to end up looking at my locker from the inside.

"You can't prove anything. You need to keep your stupid mouth shut."

"And you need to keep your stupid hands off me." I twist my body as hard as I can, somehow managing to get out of his grasp and over to the other side of the hall before he can grab me again.

"You stay away from me and everyone I know. Touch me again, and I'll call the cops so fast it will make your empty head spin." I walk off down the hall, forcing myself not to break into a run. I don't turn to see if he's following me. I just keep moving forward until I make it to class and slip in the door, hoping the teacher doesn't decide to make an example of me for being late.

* * *

"I'll tell Cody. He can gather some guys together and get him off your case. It worked last year; it'll work again," Ryan says after school when I tell him about Shawn.

"No. It's okay. There's been enough of that crap already. I think he'll back off for now. I hope so anyway."

"You should be calling the cops now. Not waiting until he does it again."

"It's his word against mine. I just have to hope he isn't quite brainless enough to make things worse for himself by actually killing me."

"Shawn is pretty devoid of brain matter."

"But smart enough to know he shouldn't have hurt Benjamin like he did. He and his buddy, Adrian. Both of them need their heads kicked in."

"I don't think the courts use that particular punishment these days. At least the cops took Cody seriously enough to start investigating."

"They haven't charged them yet."

"I guess it takes a while to get evidence. It's not like on TV where it's all tied up in an hour, including commercial breaks. Besides, this is Thompson Mills. Our cops aren't used to anything bigger than shoplifting."

"I guess that's true." I hesitate for a second and then sigh. "Benjamin is leaving tomorrow."

"I know. He told me when I visited him yesterday." Ryan sounds sympathetic.

"Oh, I didn't know you went there."

"Yeah, he actually called me. He wanted to know about the rehab center, so I filled him in. Told him who the hot physiotherapists are."

"He might have slightly different tastes than yours in that department."

Ryan laughs. "Yeah, well, I did think about that. I wouldn't know who he would consider hot anyway. I mean, the guy likes you, so there's no accounting for taste."

"Ha-ha. Very funny. At least it would be if I actually knew whether he likes me or not."

"He obviously does. You're there all the time."

"That's not what I mean. He's kind of a captive audience."

"This feels like a Clare conversation. I'm no good at this. All I know is he talked about you, and it sounds like he thinks you're…special or whatever."

"*Special or whatever*. That's reassuring."

"He's only going for six weeks. He'll be back. That's what he told me."

"He told me that too. I'm not so sure it's true."

Ryan shrugs. "No point worrying about it now. I think maybe you should get over there and say good-bye to him though."

"I know. I'm heading there now."

I walk slowly to the hospital, trying to postpone the inevitable as long as I can. But that isn't very long in this tiny town, so I'm there in a matter of minutes.

Benjamin is propped up slightly, pillows stacked behind

him. He smiles when I come in, and it squeezes my heart so much that it takes an effort to smile back.

"Like my blanket? My mom bought it for me just in case the rehab center is as white and cold as this place." He gestures down at his lap. He's covered with brightly colored rainbows dancing across soft looking material that looks like it might finally make him feel warm.

"You should have asked Ryan about that," I say.

"I forgot. There was a lot to ask about."

"Yeah, he told me he was filling you in on the hot physio-therapists." I manage to keep my voice from sounding jealous.

"Well, he tried. Not sure he knows who I would consider to be hot."

"You should meet his girlfriend. He definitely has good taste in women. Not so sure about men."

"He's your friend. So he definitely has taste." His grin makes my whole body go into self-combustion mode. I can feel my face flaring up. I stand up quickly and walk over to the other side of the room so he won't notice.

"Is there anything I can do to help you pack?" I ask, trying to sound cool and calm. There are so many things I want to say right now, and I just can't make myself do it. He has enough to worry about without me adding to it.

"No. My mom's taking care of that at home. Did you find out anything new yet?"

"About the accident? You mean since I told you who it was?" Confusion dampens the gold specs in his eyes. I told him about Shawn yesterday—only twenty-four hours ago.

"I'm sorry. I forgot what you told me. Again." He bites his lower lip. "They say it's going to get better but it's driving me nuts. It comes and goes all the time. I can remember stupid things like what I ate for breakfast, but then someone tells me something important, and it just floats out of my brain."

"It's okay. I don't mind telling you again. Cody talked to the cops. Gave them the truck driver's name and also the name of his passenger. Who probably said something to you, but we don't know for sure. Shawn was driving, and Adrian was in the passenger seat."

When he confronted me at the dumpsters last year, Shawn had a different partner in stupidity named Matt. Adrian must be his new asshole-in-training.

"Oh, yeah, I think I remember you telling me that now that you're reminding me, but I still don't remember any of it happening. Last thing that's clear is laughing at you before I took off down the hill. You were being so slow and careful, like a little old man."

"Yeah, well, you were on some kind of daredevil mission, like a circus act or something. No feet, and I think even no hands at one point. And you were either yelling or singing." *Like I told you before. Over and over.*

He looks at me, eyes lighting up.

"I remember that now! Or maybe you just told me enough times that I think I do. It's all so murky, but I have this image in my mind of me singing. I even know what song."

"Let me guess, 'Somewhere over the Rainbow'?"

"No, smart ass, I love Judy, but it's not my favorite, even

though you might think it would be, seeing as I'm the local rainbow fanatic and all."

"It would make sense." It's one of my favorites. I think I already told him that though.

"Well, I've always been partial to singing frogs, so I'm pretty sure I was belting out 'Rainbow Connection.' You know that one?"

"Yeah. Big Muppet fan." *Kermit the Frog over Judy Garland? Seriously?*

"Well, I can't sing any better than I draw, but out on the open road no one can hear me, so I usually share that one with the birds. I'm almost sure that's what I was doing. And I'm almost sure that I actually remember doing it."

"That's good!" I'm trying so hard to sound encouraging that I almost shout it.

"It would be better if I could be completely sure, not *almost*. Hey, I know! The doctor said I should try different things to trigger memory retention. Which, ironically enough, I remember her saying. Associations, that kind of thing. One thing that's supposed to work is music. So, maybe you should sing to me and it will help me remember."

"I am not going to make like Kermit and sing about rainbows in your hospital room."

"Chicken," he says, settling back against his pillows and folding his hands across the rainbows on his lap.

"Better a chicken than a frog!"

"That's fine. Your voice is probably not as good as a frog's anyway." He laughs as I stick my tongue out at him.

I can't believe we're talking about chickens and frogs when I'm not going to see him for at least six weeks. There's so much I want to say that I wouldn't even know where to start.

So I don't.

Benjamin's eyes are starting to get heavy, and I realize it's time for me to go. I don't want to say good-bye. I'm afraid if he goes back to where he came from, he'll never return. Why would he? He's going home, where people accept him, and he has all kinds of friends.

He's going back to a place where some asshole in a pickup truck isn't going to throw him into a ditch because of who he is.

"I guess I'd better go. You seem pretty tired." His eyes are just about closed. He gives me a lopsided smile.

"Yeah. I'm still on some pretty heavy drugs. Good luck with everything. Keep in touch." His words slur and his eyes close the rest of the way as I open my mouth to say something—anything—that will make this good-bye mean something. But it's too late. He's already starting to snore, which is so cute I can't stand it.

So I turn to go, looking back at him sleeping under his silly blanket once more as I walk slowly away. He looks smaller somehow, lying there like a little kid having his afternoon nap. All he needs is a teddy bear, or maybe a stuffed unicorn, to complete the picture.

My heart twists into a tight knot that isn't going to loosen anytime soon as I force my feet out the door and maybe out of his life.

nineteen

Shawn Johanssen. Just thinking about the guy makes my skin crawl so much I feel like I need a shower. I can't believe I managed to stand up to him at school without puking on his shoes.

The first time I met him, I couldn't do anything at all. He cornered me after school, ganging up on me with his lackey of the moment. I just stood there with my back against the dumpster that stinks up the back of the school, trying to keep my lunch down while being assaulted by disgusting smells that came partly from the garbage and partly from Shawn's breath blowing hot against my face. I asked him to leave me alone, trying to sound all tough and brave, but my voice was shaking so much that it was obvious I was trying not to piss myself. I tried to move away, but that just made them both laugh as they smashed me back and held me against the metal side.

They wanted to know if the rumors were true. If I was really a *fag*. They were afraid I might decide I wanted to hit on one or both of them. They almost had it right. I definitely wanted to *hit* their stupid faces so hard they'd never laugh again.

I didn't think there was any way the situation could get worse, when all of a sudden Ryan comes up behind them. I guess he was just wheeling by, and instead of ignoring us or going for help, he decided that, somehow, he was going to be able to save me from the only two people on the planet who wouldn't see anything wrong with beating up someone who can't walk.

They threatened him, and he just stared at them calmly. He didn't look scared at all, just mildly annoyed, as if a bug had flown into his face. Ryan tried to reason with them, which was obviously not the way to go with two guys who were more interested in using their fists than their brains. He managed to piss them off even more, and one of them, I can't remember which, was actually leaning on Ryan's chair, right down into his face, when all of a sudden he went flying backwards, smashing into the dumpster beside me.

Cody and the swim team to the rescue. They made those guys back off and kept them away from us for the rest of the year. I was glad to have the protection, but at the same time, it made me feel embarrassed and weak to need it in the first place. Why couldn't I have figured out a way to make those guys leave Ryan and me alone? Why was I always the one who had to be rescued?

A better question is why should anyone need to be rescued from asswipes like those guys in the first place? Why is the world like this?

So many people have made my life difficult for so many years that I've had to work at holding onto myself and not letting them make me into the kind of person who hates. It's hard enough to *be* hated thanks to ignorance and intolerance. Sending that kind of feeling back out into the world just makes everything darker somehow, as if you just took a piece of charcoal and scribbled it across a painting, obliterating the colors and turning it all to black.

But when I think about those nightmare-inducing jerks at the dumpster or in their white truck, all I can feel is hate. I want to turn into some kind of avenging hero, like one of Ryan's stone gargoyles brought to life, so that I can smash their faces in and make an example of them so that no one in this town will ever hurt anyone again.

Which is why I've decided to do something completely different.

● ● ●

"So, I've decided. I'm going to do it."

"Good for you." Ryan looks over at me for a second and then goes back to staring at his computer screen. He's been working on his story, and I'm supposed to be sketching out ideas for the novel, but the paper in front of me is covered in rainbows instead. I don't think they will fit into his narrative very well. "What exactly is it that you're going to do?"

Nice. I just made one of the biggest decisions of my life and he's not even paying attention.

"I'm going to organize a Pride parade. In Thompson Mills."

That gets his attention. He turns his chair away from the computer and stares at me. I don't blame him. It does sound like a crazy idea now that I've actually said it out loud. But I've been thinking about it almost nonstop for several days, ever since Benjamin left, so that I've managed to push endless plans for revenge against Shawn to the back of my mind. I was dwelling on thoughts of this brain-dead guy who just ruined Benjamin's life—and mine—until it was starting to poison me, making me physically ill. And it's not like I could actually do anything to him or his buddy anyway. I have to rely on the police for that, even though it's starting to seem less and less likely that they're going to manage to prove anything—unless someone can make Adrian talk. And that is extremely doubtful because he's probably more afraid of Shawn than he is of the police.

I needed something else to focus on. Something positive. Something Benjamin might think was wonderful enough to be worth coming back here for.

Benjamin and his rainbows. Like he said in his speech, rainbows are symbols of peace, diversity, and pride. Everything that can and should be good about the world.

"A Pride parade. As in a *Gay* Pride parade. In Thompson Mills. Here, in this town called Thompson Mills, not some other town called Thompson Mills where there might be more than, oh, I don't know, two people who are gay," Ryan says, while staring at me as if I just turned into Pegasus and started flying around the room.

"Stop saying Thompson Mills. It's starting to sound weird. And yes, here in this town where there are at least two people who are gay. According to Benjamin, and the law of averages, there are probably more."

"If there are more, they're hidden so far back in the closet that no parade is going to pull them out." Ryan shakes his head.

"So, you're telling me not to do it because no one is going to give a shit?"

"I didn't say that. Lots of people will give a shit. Just in the wrong way. There are a lot of people in this town who would be against a Pride parade. And that's putting it lightly."

"Like you?" I would expect this from Cody, but coming from Ryan, it's disappointing.

"No, not like *me*. I've actually been to one before, and it was really cool. But that was in the city, where there were enough supportive people that anyone who wasn't just stayed away. I'm not sure it would happen that way here."

"Well, we can't know if we don't try." I'm making an effort to sound persuasive but I know that he's right. There will be all kinds of opposition in Thompson Mills. But does that mean we should just decide it can't happen here? Is there no chance at all that Benjamin is right about the possibility of other people accepting, even supporting us?

"True, but if we *don't* try, at least we'll know there aren't any new reasons for having the crap kicked out of us."

"So you're scared." *Me too.*

"Yep. And not afraid to admit it." He sits still for a few moments, staring at his now blank computer screen. After a while he turns to me, considering. "It might be the world's most terrible idea, but I think I get why you want to do it. The parade I went to also had a group in it supporting Disability Pride. It was pretty cool."

"Disability Pride?"

"Yeah, sounds weird, doesn't it? I used to think that the whole idea of being proud of having a disability was strange, but I've talked to Clare about it a couple of times and she got me thinking that it isn't as much about being proud to be disabled as it is about being disabled and proud to be yourself. Something like that. She explains it better."

"Yeah, well, she explains most things better than you do. So, are you saying you *would* help me with this, or not? I'm getting confused."

"It *might* be doable if we can figure out a way to *not* get the crap kicked out of us. Then again, it might not be a problem seeing as it could be kind of a small parade. Just me wheeling down Main Street with a couple of gay guys wandering along beside me. If we're lucky, maybe no one will notice."

I laugh at the image that pops into my head. Me carrying a rainbow flag in one hand and pushing Ryan's chair with the other so that he can wave his own flag, while Benjamin hopefully marches along singing the "Rainbow Connection" off key.

"We could get recruits. Caleb and Lucas already talked to me and said they'd help organize and be there on the day and bring as many people as will come. You probably have people too."

"Oh yeah, I got people." He nods his head, pursing his lips and trying to look tough.

"Ha. You know what I mean."

Ryan grins. "Well, I do keep in touch with some people from my rehab days who would probably like the idea of incorporating Disability Pride into the day. And seeing as your buddy Benjamin isn't going to be able to do much for a while—and you've just taken my spot as town hero—I guess I could help you out."

"It isn't going to be easy," I state the obvious.

He grins at me. "Nothing ever is around here."

"That's true." I grin back, but his face has turned serious.

"So, have you thought about the reality of what this is going to mean for you?" he asks.

"It's going to mean a lot of things. A lot of hassles and hard work."

"That's not what I meant. I mean do you get that you will basically be coming out to the whole town if you do this?"

He's right, of course. And, of course, I've thought about it. A lot. About whether or not I'm finally ready to let the whole town know that those rumors about me are true. Whether or not I'm ready to be myself in a place where I've always tried to be someone else. Whether I'm ready to fly on my own without Benjamin here to protect me in his bubble.

But Benjamin's bubble was broken by two assholes in a truck. The least I can do is show him that I've got more courage than a couple of homophobic cowards who can't find anything better to do than assault someone who never did them, or anyone else, any harm.

So, I'm going to do it.

"Yeah, I figured that part out," I say, in answer to Ryan's question. "I'm already most of the way out, compliments of Benjamin's stone rainbow. I guess I'll have to make it official at some point or I'll just keep living a lie for the rest of forever. Either that or move away to Bainesville and never come back."

"Personally, I think I'd choose option number two. This town is full of jerks who are not going to make life easy for you. I don't want you to end up like Benjamin."

"I don't want that either. Obviously! But it's too late for that. Most of those jerks are at our school and already know. And guess what? I don't want to keep hiding from anyone anymore, and I don't want to run away."

That's a big fat lie. I would much rather run away. Just take off into the sunset on a bicycle built for two that would take Benjamin and me to somewhere we'd be able to be together… forever.

And cue the violins. I'm starting to nauseate myself with all this mushy crap about a guy who still has no idea how I actually feel because I chickened out of telling him before he left.

"Okay then. Do you have any idea how we start?" Ryan asks.

"Like I said, I've talked to Caleb and Lucas a little, and I also did some research on how to get a parade started. I know Benjamin's mom will help us with the official part. We'll have to get permission from the town council."

"That could shut us down before we start."

"I don't know. I've been reading about this, and it seems like most local councils are more afraid of the bad press that could come from saying no than the hassles of actually having the parade." To be honest, I'm not sure Thompson Mills is big enough to be worried about any kind of press.

"Okay. So, what do we do?"

"We talk to Mrs. Lee and make a presentation to the council. Then, according to this article I read, we post on social media. Let people know it's coming and that we need help organizing." It seemed simple enough when I read about it, but I'm sure it's going to be pretty complicated.

"Let all the homophobes know where to find us, you mean?" Ryan punctuates his question by raising both eyebrows until they disappear under his orange hair.

"That too. We'll just have to figure out how to deal with that part. Everyone is already on edge with the police investigating Benjamin's so-called accident. Maybe that will keep some of the heat off us." I'm hoping the cowards around here might hesitate a little before calling attention to themselves these days.

"Do you know anything about the case? How it's going?" Ryan asks.

"No, not yet. Everything around here moves so slowly, it's like it's going in reverse."

"Yeah, well, hopefully they'll at least get enough to lay charges against those assholes. Cody is still mad at me for getting him to go to the cops. He's been getting hassled by a few people who suspect it was him."

"Poor baby," I say sarcastically.

"He's not really complaining as much as I thought he would. He still seems really pissed at the whole situation. He might even help us with the parade stuff."

"Sure, we'll get him to carry a rainbow flag and blow kisses at all the guys in the crowd." I start laughing and Ryan joins in.

"Seeing as the 'crowd' will be about four people who can't find anything better to do, I guess it wouldn't be so bad."

"I'd still like to see him marching in a Pride parade, no matter how many people are there." The thought of a multicolored Cody singing about rainbows makes me smile.

"Me too!" Ryan says. "It would be worth the effort just to see that. Anyway, I have to go. Let me know when you're going to see Mrs. Lee, I'll come with you."

"Thanks. This is going to be great," I say, trying to sound enthusiastic instead of terrified.

"Or a complete disaster. Either way, it's good you want to try. Takes guts." He smiles and waves as he wheels away.

Guts.

I wish mine would stop feeling like I'm going to puke every time I think about what it'll take to make this parade idea turn into a reality.

But all I have to do is think about Benjamin lying there under his rainbow blanket, and I know that this is something that I have to do. My guts will just have to toughen up and keep my lunch down long enough to get the job done.

twenty

"Jackson Pedersen?"

I jump to my feet, bumping my chair and scraping it across the floor with a loud grating sound that makes everyone stare in my direction. Six sets of eyes are now focused on me from the front of the room. None of them look exactly welcoming, and I'm starting to think that I should be somewhere else.

"It's all right, Jack. Just take a breath and tell them what you want to do. I'm right here." Mrs. Lee speaks in a hushed voice as she touches my arm gently. The council members are still staring impatiently as they wait for me to find the words that I practiced endlessly last night with Ryan.

"You've got this. You sounded great yesterday. Just do it the way you did for my mom and me," Ryan whispers.

"I can't remember how I did it. I can't remember anything,"

I whisper back, looking behind me to where he's sitting in his wheelchair.

"We can't hear you, Mr. Pedersen," the man in the middle of the group says, sounding like those teachers I've had who made it their mission in life to make me feel small. I look toward the front guiltily, as if I've been caught passing notes during class. *Notes! Where are my notes?*

"I don't have my notes!" I hiss snake-like while patting down all of my pockets in a blind panic. Ryan reaches forward and hands me a piece of paper.

"I made a copy just in case. Not that you need them. You can probably recite this in your sleep. You'll be fine. Just go for it."

"Mr. Pedersen!" The middle guy is now starting to look pissed, like I'm holding up the show that he thinks must go on. Obviously, there are so many terribly important issues to discuss in the massive town of Thompson Mills that there isn't time to wait for me to get my act together.

Mrs. Lee gives me a sympathetic look and nods encouragingly. "Remember to address him as *Mr. Mayor*. It makes him feel important," she whispers, smiling. Mr. Mayor is actually Mr. Greenman who runs the local convenience store when he isn't pretending to run the town. He's the kind of storekeeper that assumes every kid is in there to shoplift. He makes us leave our backpacks at the front and has surveillance cameras everywhere and then has a staff person whose only job is to follow kids around just in case someone has the sudden urge to steal a pack of gum. What he doesn't know is that this only makes kids around here even more determined to rip him off just to prove they can outsmart the system.

I take the kind of breath needed to satisfy Coach Cody before he makes me dive to the bottom of the pool and then stand up straight, doing my best to hold on to the paper without trembling. I clear my throat and try to project my shaky voice. Why didn't they give me a mic?

"Mr. Mayor and members of council, I am here today to present a proposal for the creation of a Thompson Mills Pride Parade."

"A *what?*" Mr. Mayor looks at me, deep lines furrowing his forehead. I don't know if he didn't hear me or didn't understand me.

"A Pride parade." I say it more loudly, enunciating each word carefully. He still looks confused.

"Please explain further," he says.

"I...*we*..." I gesture toward Ryan and Mrs. Lee, "want to put together a Pride parade here in town this June, near the end of the month to give us time to prepare. We are asking that Main Street be closed for one hour on the date that we all agree to and also for a permit to hold a rally on the steps of the Town Hall." I'm trying to speak slowly enough that I'm understood, but at the same time fast enough to remember all of the words, so I don't have to read them.

"How many people would you expect to attend such an event?" the mayor asks, looking skeptical now instead of confused.

"I don't actually know. Probably not very many as this

would be the first year here. We would advertise on social media and hopefully have an idea before the date."

"A Pride parade. A Gay Pride parade is what you are referring to?" Another council person is speaking now, and I look at her. I can't tell from her expression what she thinks of the idea.

"For the most part, yes. June is Gay Pride month. Many towns and cities in this area have parades in June and July." *Many* might be an exaggeration, but there are definitely a few. I have the names written down on my paper just in case they ask.

"We also want to incorporate Disability Pride into the day," Ryan speaks up from behind me. He wheels his chair out and into the aisle so they can see him better. A couple of councilors nod and smile. One even waves. Ryan is pretty well-known in our town, the combination of bright orange hair and wheelchair making him more visible than most people.

"Disability Pride? I don't think I've heard of that." The mayor purses his lips, as if we must be making it up if he hasn't heard of it.

"Pride is about acceptance. Accepting yourself and everyone around you. Pride parades celebrate everything that makes us different and everything that makes us the same." Mrs. Lee stands up as she speaks. Her voice commands the whole room and all of the councilors look at her like well-behaved school kids afraid to piss off the principal.

"All preparations and materials required will be coordinated through the high school, so we aren't asking for any funding at this time. We are simply seeking the cooperation of this council and the option of a brief closure of Main Street."

"I'm not sure what purpose there would be to such an event here." The mayor puts a slight emphasis on the word *here*.

"Why not here? Is there some reason Thompson Mills doesn't want to recognize Pride Month?" The words come shooting out of my mouth, flinging toward the row of faces with a force that surprises everyone, especially me.

"I wasn't aware that we had…a *community* that would be interested," the mayor says, tiptoeing around my question.

"Is that code for you trying to say you weren't aware that we have any *gay* people here? Well, I'm gay. Mrs. Lee's son, Benjamin, is gay. And who knows how many other people there are here who are afraid to admit it because this town makes it impossible to be different. After what happened to Benjamin Lee, we need to do something to let people know that Thompson Mills has some hope for the future. That we can have a town that is safe for anyone and everyone to live in." I'm improvising, and I can't keep track of my own words. I can feel my face warming up, so I sit down quickly before they notice my flushed cheeks.

"Thompson Mills has an excellent safety record. A very low crime rate," Mr. Mayor says pompously. A couple of councilors nod in agreement. One woman closes her eyes for a second and just shakes her head.

"That isn't what he's saying," she says, looking at him and then over at me. "Is it?"

"No," I say quietly, shaking my head.

"Mr. Pedersen isn't talking about crime, although recent events have made it clear to me that issues in this town have escalated. I believe, and please feel free to correct me, that Mr. Pedersen is referring to feeling safe from intolerance. Wanting to live in a town where everyone is accepted for who they are as individuals. Is that close?" She looks at me again.

"Yes."

The mayor glares at the council woman. She might be the mother of one of the kids on my old soccer team, but I'm not totally sure.

"Recent events, as you call them, would make it seem that this *isn't* the time for this sort of thing. The atmosphere is not really one of…" He hesitates.

"Acceptance? Tolerance? Basic respect?" Mrs. Lee punches each word out into the room. "I would think that *recent events*—a polite way of saying that my son was injured in what was most likely a deliberate attempt to frighten him because he's gay—would be exactly the reason that this parade is desperately needed. The *atmosphere* needs to be changed."

"We will take your request under advisement and get back to you shortly with a decision. Thank you for your presentation," the mayor says abruptly, sounding extremely annoyed and obviously telling us to get the hell out. We are supposed to thank the council for their time before leaving, but I don't really see what I have to thank them for. Obviously, Mrs. Lee and Ryan agree because we all head out in silence.

Once we get downstairs and out onto the sidewalk, I look up at the building.

"Do you think there's a chance?" I ask Mrs. Lee.

"I think there's every chance. They actually can't deny the right to a peaceful assembly, so no matter what happens here, we can figure out a way to have a gathering. The question will be whether or not they will allow the road closure and use of the Town Hall grounds. Also, whether or not they will officially endorse the parade as a town function."

"I'm not sure what that last part means."

"Well, they can allow the parade but distance themselves from it. I read of that happening in other places. The local government chooses not to include the event on the official town calendar, for example, and in some cases even takes out an ad making it clear that it does not support the function. It's a way of meeting basic rights requirements without actually having to be supportive. I would imagine that would be the route chosen by *Mr. Mayor Greenman*." Mrs. Lee drips puddles of sarcasm down onto each word.

"It sounds like bullshit to me," Ryan says.

"Ryan!" I point at Mrs. Lee, the vice principal of our school. He looks up at her and grins.

"Oops. Sorry about that. Please don't tell my mom I just did that. She'd be less than impressed, even though I was just saying it like it is. By the way, she's all over helping with this. She said she'd get her school involved with making posters and things like that."

"Isn't she afraid that parents will get pissed if little kids are making posters for a bunch of gay people?" I ask.

"No. She said it fits with something called the 'social justice' curriculum. She also doesn't give a shi…" He stops and smiles at Mrs. Lee. "Doesn't *care* what parents think when it comes to something she believes in, like this."

"You did a wonderful job, Jackson."

"I'm not so sure about that. I forgot some things. And I was supposed to say LGBTQ+ but I just kept using *gay*."

"Greenman was having enough trouble with the word *gay*. He would have passed out if he'd had to try to figure out what the rest of it means."

Mrs. Lee smiles at Ryan and turns to me. "You spoke very well, quite impassioned. I should have filmed it for Benjamin. He is so excited you're doing this," Mrs. Lee says.

"Thanks, but I don't think it was video-worthy. You did more than I did."

"Well, I disagree on both points. I'm proud of you, and Benjamin will be proud too, when I tell him about it. I'm going to do that right now, if you'll both excuse me."

"Thanks for coming with us. It really helped," I tell her.

"You are most welcome, but I think you would have been just fine on your own. Good night, boys. You are quite remarkable young men. I'm glad Benjamin is friends with you both."

Friends. Thanks to Shawn, Asshole of the Century, we didn't get a chance to see if we could turn it into something more than that. We didn't even finish our first date.

We watch her walk off and then head home ourselves. I feel like we should be talking about what just went down, but I can't find any more words. I'm drained, as if I just swam a marathon with Cody yelling at me the whole time.

"So, how does it feel?" Ryan asks, breaking several minutes of silence.

"I feel tired," I answer, sighing a little for emphasis.

"That's not what I meant. I mean, how does it feel to officially stand there in an official meeting with official-looking people staring at you and officially come out."

"It feels…very official."

He laughs. "But seriously, are you okay?"

"Actually, I'm good. I mean, it's not like everyone didn't already know."

"It's still different to actually come out and say it."

"Come *out* and say it?" I grin at him and he laughs again.

"I guess that's exactly what you did."

I stop walking and just stand there. I can see the bridge at the end of the street, looking tired and worn but still proudly guarding the river the way it's done for so long that no one can remember a time that it wasn't standing there. The water is excited today, just enough of a breeze floating in that I can see movement in the late afternoon sun, little sparks of light reflecting off the gentle waves. The birds drift in and out of the trees, filling the air with their version of singing as the wildflowers dance cheerfully, happy to be back in full bloom again.

It looks the same as it always has. Everything does.

But nothing is ever going to be the same again.

Because I just made it official.

I'm gay.

And I don't care what the council decides.

I'm going to make a rainbow parade.

twenty-one

I'm sitting on my bed trying to force myself to get up and get moving. I've been awake for at least two hours, maybe more, and it's only six-thirty now. I seem to be glued to the mattress, destined to spend all eternity looking at my boring green walls.

The town council approved the plan but modified it from what we asked for. We can use the Town Hall steps for a rally, but we don't get road closure for the parade part. The assumption is that the crowd will be small enough to stick to the sidewalks. We can advertise on social media, but the town isn't going to advertise at all. Mrs. Lee called that one right. The mayor is obviously not a fan, so he basically said we could have a parade as long as we don't call it the Thompson Mills Pride Parade. We can say it's *in* Thompson Mills though. A small but apparently important distinction.

We decided to have it on the Saturday before grad, which

is on a Tuesday night. Clare and Lucas and maybe Caleb will be coming down anyway, because they wanted to watch us graduate, so they're going to come early and help.

Today is the day Mrs. Lee is going to make the announcement to the school, which right now feels less than great. She's going to tell the entire population of TMHS that I am planning a Pride parade and that anyone interested in volunteering can come to a meeting at lunchtime to sign up. I am going to have to sit in the art room with no other students but Ryan beside me for the whole lunch period, waiting for no one to come. Then I'm going to have to walk down the halls while everyone stares and points and whispers and laughs. And probably a few other things that I'm not going to bother thinking about right now.

Not that I'll find that part particularly new or different. It's been my life for so long, I'm almost used to it. *Almost* being the operative word. I don't think anyone actually gets used to being treated like a pariah.

I'm not sure Ryan is going to enjoy it much. He *is* used to being different. He's told me before that some people stare at him in a way that makes it seem like they think he's contagious or something. Other people are overly sympathetic, treating him like he has something fatal and needs tender loving care. But for the most part, people are pretty decent with him. No one thinks he's perverted or sick.

That might change for him today. Everyone knows we're friends, but actually helping the gay kid with a Pride parade lifts that relationship to a whole new level. "You don't have to do it, you know. I can handle it. Mrs. Lee is going to be here," I told him last night, trying to give him a chance to escape before he got in too deep to get back out again.

He looked at me for a few seconds, head tilted a little to the side like he was trying to figure something out. Looking for something that he couldn't see straight on.

"You're trying to protect me now? Turning the tables? That's nice, but I'm a big boy. I said I'd do it, and I'm going to."

"Okay. It's just, you don't really get what it might turn into, the kind of crap people could decide to shove at you. It will be different."

"I've had more crap shoved my way than most people realize. It's not exactly been a picnic in the park. I've been the only kid in a wheelchair my whole life. No one in this town has ever had even the slightest idea of what my life has been like. And I prefer it that way. My personal life is my own business. But I'm not some wimp who can't take an insult or even a threat. I've spent years coping with Cody, after all."

He smiled a little, but his eyes stayed serious. Ryan is always so tough and sure of himself that I don't often think about the types of challenges that come his way. How hard life as the only wheelchair-bound person in a high school might be. I've seen what it's like for him to deal with stores that don't have automatic doors and buildings without ramps, but I don't know how it feels. I complain that my dad doesn't respect my soccer skills and would laugh if he knew I love to dance. But Ryan doesn't even have the option of trying those things. He has swimming, but he can't just decide that he'd rather do hockey instead. At least not here.

"You're right. Anyone who deals with Cody as well as you do can handle anything. Speaking of Cody, can I ask you a personal question?"

"If you really have to." Ryan looked at me a little warily, which is fair, seeing as he'd just finished saying that his personal life is his own business.

"Well, I've noticed that you don't mind Cody helping out with physical things, but you seem really uncomfortable if I offer to do anything for you. As in, you basically tell me to get lost if I try. I was just wondering why." I asked the question even though I wasn't sure I wanted to know his answer. He looked at me with a puzzled expression before saying anything.

"I never really thought about it before. I guess Cody is the only one outside of my family that I feel comfortable with." He shrugged slightly.

"So, it isn't just me?"

"No, not at all. I don't let anyone help me if I can avoid it. But I've known Cody a long time, and he's always just stepped in and done stuff for me without asking, and it just became… natural, I guess. I like to be independent, and when anyone else but Cody or family steps up, I feel like I'm not in control. I'm sorry if I upset you."

"No, don't be sorry. I wasn't upset. Just curious. I guess Cody can be…helpful when he wants to be."

"Cody can be a lot of things to a lot of people. He's a complicated guy." Ryan grinned a little.

"Yeah, that's one word for him!" I laughed. "Anyway, changing the topic back. You definitely think you're ready for whatever's going to happen tomorrow?"

"Ready to sit in a classroom and wait for no one? Sure." He grinned full on.

"My art teacher will be there, seeing as it's her room, and Mrs. Lee, of course. But I doubt there will be any kids other than us."

"It doesn't matter who comes. We can make a few posters ourselves and we'll have stuff from my mom's school also. Clare and everyone will be here at least the day before and she's into crafts. Not to mention Lucas, who probably has a whole Pride-parade-in-a-box or something like that. I also heard from a few guys from my rehab days who are interested, and I could ask them to bring some signs or whatever. It's all good."

● ● ●

It's all good. That's what he said yesterday.

Except that now it's today and I have to get my butt off this bed and face the music. Which is not the right expression to be using, because I like music. I'd much rather be facing an orchestra than the kids at my school.

Maybe I should lie down for a few minutes and just relax before trying to get moving. Try to dream a little and forget about everything.

I just manage to close my eyes and lie back when my tablet starts pinging at me.

Clare must be calling! That's perfect. She always knows exactly what to say to me when I'm being a chickenshit.

I sit up, reaching over to grab my tablet. I accept the call quickly, so she doesn't slip away. I sit back and watch for her face to appear on the screen.

"*Nǐ hǎo.*"

I stare openmouthed at Benjamin's big brown eyes looking at me. I was in such a hurry that I didn't even check to see if it was actually Clare.

"What?" I finally manage to get a sound out. He grins at me, and I start to melt like the Wicked Witch of the West.

"Just saying hey. My grandparents are rubbing off on me. You look surprised to see me. Did I wake you up?" I pull myself out of puddle mode and shake my head.

"No, I've been awake for a while. I just thought you were Clare."

"Clare?" He looks puzzled.

"Ryan's girlfriend."

"Oh, right. Why would you think I was her?" He still looks confused.

"Oh, well, I just chat with her sometimes. And her brother too." I tack that on quickly. I'm not sure why.

"I hope you're not disappointed it's me then."

"No! Not at all!" I accidentally shout at the screen. He laughs a little and my cheeks start to betray me. Hopefully he's on his phone and the picture will be small enough that he won't notice.

"Well, I was just calling to wish you luck. Mom told me today is the big day."

"I don't know how big it will be. Probably just me, Ryan and your mom sitting in the art room staring at each other."

"That's not what I mean by big. I mean it's a big deal that you're doing it at all. The first time I suggested it to you, it was obvious that you thought I was nuts."

"Yeah, well, it is kind of nuts. But it feels like the right thing to do. To try to do, anyway."

"I love the theme. *Rainbows Reign.* It's a great slogan. It's everything the parade is meant to be."

"I thought so. I didn't make it up though. I found it online."

"It's perfect. The whole thing will be awesome. I've already talked to a bunch of kids here, and they all want to come down for it."

"I've created the event posting, and Ryan shared it last night so more people will see it. Your mom is sharing it on the school page later today. Clare will share it today too, and that will get it out into Bainesville."

"I saw it this morning. I didn't know you were going to actually dedicate the whole thing to me. It kind of choked me up. Then again, I'm pretty emotional these days, so most things have that effect."

"Well, I never would have thought of doing anything like this if it wasn't for you."

"If I hadn't got myself tossed into the ditch, you mean?"

"No, I don't mean that. Well, not totally. That is part of it. I wanted to do something special for you after what you went through…are still going through. But also, it's because you made me think about…having the courage to be myself, I guess." Now I sound like the cowardly lion at the end of the movie. Next, I'll start dancing around looking for a brain.

"It's nice of you to give me credit, but I'm pretty sure it was always in there. I shared the post and asked my friends to share it too. It's getting around. You might be surprised when you start checking the response."

"As of this morning, there were five people going."

"It's six-forty. Give it some time!" He laughs.

"I guess. Why are you up so early?"

"Oh, my sleep is a bit screwed up. They changed my meds a couple of days ago and it's affecting my system a bit."

"I hate that you have to deal with all of this. I wish this hadn't happened to you."

"Me too. And I still can't remember exactly what did happen, but my memory is getting better every day, so maybe eventually it'll come to me."

"I don't think I'd want to remember something like that."

"I know. Sometimes I think it's a good thing. But it feels strange to have this…black hole in my mind. I want to know what they said to me, if anything. What pissed them off so much that they tried to hurt me. *If* they tried to hurt me, that is."

"You must be glad to be away from Thompson Mills." The words are out there and now I can't take them back, even though I'm wishing I hadn't said them.

"It's nice to be back home. But there are things I miss about Thompson Mills." He smiles but doesn't say anything more.

Am I one of the things he misses? Would Clare tell me to say something? There should be an app for this.

"So, how does your mom feel about all of this?" he asks.

Great. I sat here so long that he changed the subject.

"Actually, she's been surprisingly supportive, seeing as it's so public. I think Ryan's mom might have done some persuading there. Mom's worried that my dad might find out though. He lives pretty far from us, and we never see him anymore, but she's worried that somehow we'll be so famous that he'll see it," I answer, still wondering how to find a way to ask him if he misses me.

"Are you worried?" I look at him, considering the question. *Am I worried?* If my dad somehow found out Thompson Mills was having a Pride parade and was interested enough to check it out and then somehow found out that I'm organizing it, and on top of all that was smart enough to deduce I'm gay...well, I guess if he did all that, I'd just have to deal with it. And so would he. But the odds are definitely against it happening.

"No." I give him the short answer.

"Good. So, Mom said no floats this year. Just a march with posters and flags?"

"Yeah. It'll be enough to do that much. She's ordering a few real flags, and we're going to make the rest. We're going to do the rally, too. Lucas is going to speak and maybe Caleb. Maybe me, if I get up the guts."

"You could also think about some entertainment for the rally part to spice it up a bit. Like, maybe a singer?" His eyes become not so subtle laser pointers.

"Me? You're looking at me? No way, I don't sing in public.

The closest I've ever come to that is down at the bridge, and then it's only birds listening to me."

"I bet you sound really good. You probably don't know how talented you are. Art and music. You told me you like dancing too, right? Triple threat."

"I mostly dance in my head. Besides, I don't think those are the three things most people mean when they talk about triple threat." I should tell him about Ryan's "misogynistic, homophobic, and relatively racist" definition. Then again, seeing as Benjamin's sitting in a rehab center right now because of one of those Thompson Mills' triple threats, he probably already knows.

"I mostly dance in my head these days too." He looks down, I assume at the legs that still aren't holding him up.

"How is the therapy going?"

"They said there's no permanent damage to my spine. My hip is healing well enough that we've started physio, but I'm still in this chair for a bit to keep the weight off everything for a while longer. Too bad I'm not still in Thompson Mills. Ryan would have someone to wheel around town with for a change."

Is that what he misses about Thompson Mills? Ryan? I want to ask it out loud but I don't...just in case.

"He'd probably like that. But they aren't thinking you'll still need one by the time you come back here, are they?"

"According to the staff here, it's all up to me. How hard I decide to work—blah, blah. No matter what, I'm coming back for the parade, even if I have to wheel my way down the sidewalk. And I want to be there for grad, too."

"It will be pretty lame here compared to your school." I assumed that he would decide to just stay there and graduate with his friends.

"I'm still looking forward to it. I thought I might be able to persuade you to go to the dance with me, seeing as everyone assumes we're a couple anyway."

The world stops spinning for a moment as my smile stretches across my face until my lips feel like they're about to touch my ears.

"Really?" The *y* squeaks out, catching in the back of my throat and making me cough a little. Benjamin laughs.

"Yes, really. I figured you'd never get up the guts to ask me, so I was going to jump the gun before I even came here. I just wasn't sure if you were ready to be that far out in public yet."

"Well, the council meeting was a pretty big push, and I'm going to be the rest of the way out in about…" I look at the time, "…three hours, give or take. There won't be any turning back then. Everyone has been thinking it for so long, especially since Rainbow-gate, that I don't think anyone will react that much anyway."

"Rainbow-gate?" he asks. I laugh self-consciously.

"That's what Ryan calls the art project day when you outed yourself at school and brought me along for the ride."

"I guess this is where I'm supposed to say I'm sorry. But I'm not."

He gives me the world's sexiest grin and my tongue ties itself into knots while my face flares up as if I just stuck it in front of a hot fire on a cold winter's day. Actually, I'm so hot and bothered that it feels like I jumped right into the fire. I seriously have to develop some self-control or I'm actually going to self-combust, which could mess up any plans I might have of going to the dance with Benjamin.

"Anyway, I'd better let you go and kick some ass. You're going to be great. I'll talk to you later and you can tell me how awesome it was," Benjamin says after a few seconds when it becomes obvious that I'm not going to say anything. I just nod, still not sure I can trust my voice as he disappears from view.

I can't believe he asked me to the dance. That is the single most amazing and terrifying thing that's ever happened to me.

Shit. I don't think I even remembered to say yes!

twenty-two

I managed to cool down a little but still walked around feeling pretty warm and fuzzy until exactly 11:47 a.m., which was one minute ago. Now I'm sitting here, basically waiting for nothing, just like I imagined I would be. Ryan's on my right, Mrs. Lee's on my left, and my art teacher, Ms. Cameron, is at the back of the room marking students' work while waiting for a meeting that might never start.

"Told you," I say to Ryan, as if somehow this is on him. He just rolls his eyes at me.

"Class let out exactly eight minutes ago. People could barely get here in that amount of time."

"We've been here for five."

"Give it a few more minutes before you panic completely. Besides, we decided it doesn't matter who shows up. We have enough help. My parents, Mrs. Lee, and Ms. Cameron, for a start. Your mom, too. She told my mother that she'd work on the DIY flags with her at our place."

"Really? She didn't tell me that she was doing that." That's a surprise. She hasn't exactly told me not to do this, but she hasn't been jumping for joy either, and definitely hasn't been offering to help.

"She wanted it to be a surprise…and that's why I wasn't supposed to say anything. Oops." Ryan grins sheepishly but doesn't look particularly sorry.

"That's okay. I'm glad I know. At least someone wants to help." I look at my phone—again. Eleven fifty. Lunch only runs another half hour.

"It's going to be fine, Jack," Mrs. Lee says from where she's been working on her laptop. "No matter who does or doesn't show up here."

She's right. He's right. It doesn't matter if anyone from this backward-thinking, stuck-in-the-Dark-Ages, intolerant, pathetic school—

"Hi! Is this the parade meeting?" A voice interrupts my internal rant. Sarah Edey is standing at the door with two buddies. Right behind her are about five more girls I recognize from my art class.

Eight people! Standing right here. For my meeting. For my *Pride parade* meeting. I take it all back.

"Yeah, come on in," Ryan says when he realizes that I'm counting people with my mouth hanging open and no sound coming out.

"Hi, Ryan. Hi, Jack. Hi, Mrs. Lee," Sarah says, sitting

down and folding her hands, looking at me expectantly. I feel like I should start teaching a lesson on illustrious abstract artists, or something eloquent like that, instead of discussing the different sizes of rainbows I want to draw.

"Hi, Sarah. I'm pleased to see you here. All of you," Mrs. Lee says warmly, nodding at everyone.

"Thanks, Mrs. Lee. We wanted to help when we saw Jack's Facebook post that said the parade was being dedicated to Benjamin. We all feel terrible about what happened to him." Sarah looks around at the rest of the girls.

"Definitely. I mean, everyone has their own opinion about things, but no one has the right to hurt someone else. Benjamin is such a nice guy." The girl next to Sarah—I think her name is Nancy—looks over at me and smiles.

"I watch lots of TV shows with gay characters, and they all seem cool. It's just…around here it's never really been okay to admit that. At least, not with the kids I know." Sarah shrugs, looking a little uncomfortable.

"Well, you're here now, and that's the important thing," Mrs. Lee says. "There's lots of work to be done, and we can use all the help we can get."

"I think we can find a few more people for next time. It's just that no one was sure about being the first to step up, you know?" Nancy says.

"Now that you did, we'd better get started. Jack, I'll turn it over to you." Mrs. Lee gets up and goes to the back of the group. I stand there for a few seconds, looking at the eight girls and Ryan. Nine people who want to help me make rainbows for my parade. My eyes water a little, probably from the paint fumes in here. *Right.*

"Okay, well, we have a few weeks to get this organized. Mostly we need to make some posters and come up with some other creative ways to get noticed. The theme is obviously Pride, but as I said in the post, we're going to use Rainbows Reign as our main slogan, so we're going to really focus on rainbows, both in the flags and on the posters and everything else to honor Benjamin. His project is sitting on the shelf at the back of the classroom, so if you aren't in our art class and don't know the symbolism of the rainbow and significance of the colors, you can check it out there. There's a typed explanation beside it in a folder. But basically, the rainbow represents peace, harmony, and diversity. All things we want to talk about in Thompson Mills." I look back at Benjamin's stone rainbow. It still amazes me every time I see it. It looks like something out of an art gallery to me. And he says I'm the artistic one!

"So, what do you want us to do now?" Sarah asks.

"I thought we could use today as a brainstorming session. Think about what kinds of things we want to carry. Check out some other slogans and things online that would work. Then we can come back and figure out what we need to actually start putting things together." I look over at Mrs. Lee for approval, and she gives me a thumbs up.

"So, just take a few minutes to talk about ideas and look at Benjamin's project if you need to. You can ask questions, but I probably won't have any answers." Everyone laughs. I was going for honest, not funny, but the laughter still sounds nice. For the first time I get that whole "they're laughing with you, not at you" thing that my mother always said to me when I was younger.

"I can't believe this!" I say to Ryan as we watch the girls talking away, looking at Benjamin's project, and reading things on their phones that might even relate to what we're doing. Or they might just be checking text messages. Who cares? They're here and willing to help.

"It's cool. I thought some girls might show. I figured guys would be too chicken."

"Fine with me. Anyone is better than no one."

"Clare would love this. She told me they are going to bring some of their own signs and flags and things from Bainesville. They have a Rainbow Club at her school and they've decided to double-up this year and work on our parade and theirs at the same time."

"That's incredible. I feel a bit like I'm dreaming and I'm afraid to wake up." I should pinch myself just to be sure.

"You're not the only one! We must both be dreaming. Check it out." Ryan points over toward the door of the classroom. I actually have to pinch myself when I see who's standing there, leaning ever so casually against the doorframe as if he shows up at Pride meetings every day of the week.

I would have said there wasn't a snowball's chance in hell that we'd ever see Cody McNeely at a Pride meeting, but here he is. He looks over at us and saunters into the room, stopping to flirt with each one of the girls as he passes by.

"Hey," he says.

"Hey," Ryan answers, the look on his face a cross between shocked and ready to burst out laughing.

"Hey," I say it too, which sounds silly all of a sudden, and I have to bite down on my lower lip to keep it from smiling.

"So. I don't paint. I don't draw. I don't do rainbows, period." Cody looks at me sternly as if I had asked him to do all of those things.

"Okaaay…." I don't want to say the wrong thing so I just keep it short.

"So, why the hell are you here then?" Ryan asks, obviously not worried about what he says.

"Well, I figured that this deal might need…security. You know, keep the assholes at bay."

"I was hoping they'd just decide to stay home that day," I say.

He looks at me like I'm three years old and just peed myself in public. "Dream on, lover boy. There'll be enough guys around here who want to hassle you."

"The police might be able to help out," Ryan says, even though we already know that the official line is that the police won't be formally assigned to the parade that day.

"The cops who still haven't figured out how to charge Shawn even though I put my reputation on the line to rat him out? Don't think they'll be much help. So, I am offering security for the day." He folds his arms, looking tough. But not tough enough to hold off hordes of hassling homophobes on his own.

"If you're right and people are planning to hassle us, do you think *you're* enough to stop them?" Ryan asks. Cody looks annoyed to say the least.

"I would be enough for anyone, but these guys insisted on coming along." He gestures toward the door. The rest of the swim team is standing at the back of the room, looking monumentally uncomfortable, along with four or five other big guys I recognize but don't actually know.

"I got our guys and a few of the football squad who had the balls to step up," Cody says. "They're ready to help on condition that we don't have to come to your rainbow meetings. I'll talk to you guys and organize the security detail directly with them. Deal?"

"Yeah, absolutely!"

He looks me in the eye for a second and then holds out his hand. I manage not to wince as I grasp his hand and he squeezes my fingers in a death grip as we shake. He smiles slightly and then saunters back out of the room, like some kind of mafia don with his goon squad following close behind him.

I really hope we don't need them. But it's about ten degrees past amazing that we have them.

I examine my hand, which is still more or less intact after Cody's handshake. I can't believe he actually touched me in front of the entire swim team and half of the football team, not to mention a group of girls!

And he did it so that we could agree on his offer to help with a rainbow themed parade that I'm planning in honor of a gay guy whose dad was born in China.

Maybe Cody isn't as much of a triple threat as he used to be.

twenty-three

"I can't believe this! There are already fifty people who are *definitely going* and another twenty *maybes!*" I'm staring at the screen in absolute amazement. The post has only been up for a few days and I have at least fifty comments and sixty *likes.* The event page has been viewed more than a hundred times. This is so much better than I'd expected.

"Well, what did you expect? You're doing something marvelous and people are responding. And I would imagine this is just the tiny tip of the iceberg. There's a whole world outside of Thompson Mills." Lucas smiles at me with crimson lips parted over perfectly straight, blindingly white teeth. His eyelashes are gold tipped today, which reminds me of Benjamin. Then again, pretty much everything reminds me of Benjamin—who asked me to the dance.

Oh, my god! He asked me to the dance! I've been so busy recently that I haven't taken the time to fully process it.

I still can't remember if I answered him. What if he thinks I don't want to go with him? Even though the prospect of going to a dance in Thompson Mills with a guy is terrifying on every possible level, there is no way I could turn Benjamin down. I'm braver than that.

I really hope that's true.

"Earth to Jackie. Are you in there?" Lucas calls out, making a knocking gesture toward the screen.

"Oh, sorry. I was just thinking."

"Judging from the look in those big dark eyes of yours, you weren't thinking about me." He grins, fluttering those golden eyelashes at me suggestively. He knows about Benjamin asking me to the dance. I had to tell someone about it—*someone* being Clare, of course—and she asked if she could tell Lucas because he's the world's biggest romantic, and she figured he would be thrilled for me. She figured right.

"No, I was thinking about who I'm always thinking about. I can't believe he actually asked me out!"

"Well, you are just so adorably naïve then. It's been obvious that he's into you for quite a while from everything you've said about him. You just haven't been reading the signals."

"I wouldn't know a signal if it jumped up and bit me."

"Mmmm—that would be fun!" he says in a voice that sounds like a cat purring. It makes me blush.

"You know what I mean. No one has ever sent me any before. Everything about this is so new."

"How lovely for you. The first time is so sweet. I still remember mine. I couldn't eat for a week. Lost three pounds. Which reminds me…" He stands up and steps back from the screen. "Do you like?" he asks, twirling around to show me a tight, gold-colored dress that matches his lashes. "I've been watching my carbs and I just got back into this. Jamal is going to pass out when he sees me!"

"You look beautiful. Jamal's a lucky guy."

"So is Benjamin. Maybe we could get you into something pretty for that dance."

I look at him and sigh. I would love to try wearing something pretty for the dance. Maybe not skin-tight gold, but something a bit more daring than my usual masquerade of jeans and a T-shirt might be nice.

"I think Thompson Mills will already be reeling from the parade. It's way more than enough to add a gay couple at grad without dressing it up too much."

"Well, I disagree, but there's always time to make you change your mind."

That would be nice but I'm not sure I can. I'm still keeping that part of me away from my mother, even though Matthew thinks I should just let it all hang out. I am pretty positive that accepting me in a dress and makeup would be even harder for Mom than the idea that I am hoping to have sex with a guy someday. She's still struggling enough with that. I'm not sure she could handle anything more right now. She never mentioned her missing skirt, and I find it hard to believe she didn't notice it was gone because she's not exactly a clothes horse, or whatever the expression is. But I have no idea if she would guess that I'm the one who took it. Maybe she thinks my dad stole it when he left, just to be mean or something. I don't know. I just figure if she doesn't ask, I don't have to tell.

I wonder what Benjamin would think if I ever had the guts to let Lucas give me that makeover he keeps offering? Lucas tells me that he can take my inner beauty and put it on the outside, so everyone can see it. Would Benjamin think I'm beautiful or would it make everything awkward? He likes colorful clothes more than most guys around here, but I'm pretty sure that's as far as it goes. The way the girls still look at him, you'd think he'd never come out at all.

I know that clothes are just the wrapping paper and not the gift inside—mostly because I read it on Twitter—but I'd still love the chance to break out a few ribbons and bows someday. The only thing is, I'm not sure how Benjamin would feel about me if I ever had the guts to dress the way I do in my dreams.

"I'm scared there's time for *him* to change his mind. That I'll do something stupid and he'll decide he doesn't want to go out with me after all. Or someone else will do something terrible on parade day and he'll just want to get the hell away from Thompson Mills and everything that reminds him of it."

"You won't do anything stupid. And as for anyone else, just surround yourself with friends. You have them, you know. Keep them close." Lucas's face turns serious and sympathetic at the same time. I look at him for a few seconds and then take a deep breath.

"I'm just scared of so many things. I'm afraid of how

people will react to the parade and to me being such a big part of it. I feel sick every time I imagine how people might react to Benjamin and me walking into that dance together, even though I want to go with him more than anything in the world. I'm afraid to dress the way I feel, partly because I don't know if my mom could handle it, but I'm even more afraid that I'll never have the guts to do it. It all just spins around inside of me until I start to feel dizzy. How do I stop feeling this way?"

"Oh, sweet boy, I don't know if you can stop completely until the rest of the world catches up and just realizes that there isn't anything to fear from letting people love whoever they want to love." He grins at me. "Someday love *will* win if we don't let fear get the upper hand. In the meantime, you just push it down, deep enough inside that you can live your life the way you want to. Someday you'll go looking for it and realize it's buried too deep for you to find anymore."

"That's beautiful. You should be a writer."

He laughs. "Thanks. I guess Clare never told you about my blog. Anyway, you are well on your way. Look at what you've accomplished already. You're creating a Pride Day. You're falling in love. You are amazing."

Falling in love. Is that what this is? This obsessed wondering about what Benjamin might be doing every minute of the day?

I wasn't sure if I was falling in love or just stalking him with my mind.

"But what if we do actually start going out and then Benjamin changes his mind about me some day?"

"You'll deal with it. We all do. I've fallen in and out of love a few times and it's the most wonderful and terrifying feeling in the world. But you just have to keep trying. Jamal isn't my first love, but I think he's going to be my last." He holds his hand up to the screen, so close that it's blurry at first and I can't see what I'm looking at. He shifts it just enough that I realize I'm looking at a diamond ring.

"Lucas! That's great!"

"Isn't it though? So beautiful. I had one made for him too, but much more subtle. Jamal is a little more conservative than me."

"Mardi Gras is more conservative than you."

He laughs. "Why you sweetheart! Thank you. I have to agree. I also have to go. I have a hot date. I'm proud of you, Jackie. I am so looking forward to the twenty-fifth."

He blows me a kiss and fades from the screen.

The twenty-fifth. Two weeks from now. Time is flying by so fast that I can't catch up to it. We've been working almost every day and have a pile of posters, flags, and various rainbows ready to go. There are a few crowns and scepters there too, because Sarah thought they would go nicely with the idea of rainbows actually reigning. It's one of those slogans that needs some visuals just in case people think we're expecting rainbows to start falling out of the clouds. Sarah and Nancy managed to rope a few more of their friends into helping, and it's been fun hanging out in the art room getting creative.

Not everyone is happy with our plans, obviously. The population of Thompson Mills hasn't been replaced by clones.

We've had quite a few negative comments online that I deleted immediately. Some guys at school are still glaring at me and sometimes following me around trying to be terrifying, but that isn't really working anymore.

My mom is coming around. I even heard her shoot down a couple of customers at the restaurant who were badmouthing the parade. She was so fierce that I almost felt sorry for them. I bet she didn't get a tip.

The town council is mostly ignoring us, although Mrs. Lee said we're going to go back and speak with them if the numbers keep rising. There's no guarantee it will change their minds about closing the road. I think this will be a case of seeing is believing.

Benjamin calls me every day now. We talk about the parade and his progress, movies and books, life in general. It's the best fifteen minutes of my day.

He's looking stronger all the time. He took a few steps yesterday, with support. He said it hurt, but it felt great to be up. He's still planning on being here in two weeks, with or without a wheelchair.

"Jack—phone!" my mom calls up to me. I put my tablet on the bed and run downstairs. We still have a landline because my mom is so old school that she doesn't like cell phones, but no one ever calls me on it.

"Who is it?" I mouth to her as I come into the room. She just shakes her head and hands me the phone.

"Hello?"

"Jack Pedersen?"

"Yes."

"This is Officer Peabody. We met last year. Do you remember me?"

"Yes." How could I forget the cop who showed up to question me after Ryan's big save? What does *she* want?

"I'm calling to let you know that we have just charged Shawn Johanssen. We will need your testimony when the case comes to trial."

"Charged him? With what?"

"I can only share the public data, which is that the charge is currently dangerous driving. We will need your eye witness account of what you saw that day."

"I told you before I'm not sure what they were doing."

"All we need from you is to tell us what you did see. They'll take it from there."

"Okay. When?"

"It takes a while for cases to come to court. As soon as a date is set and the lawyers are ready to speak with you, we will let you know."

"All right."

"Thank you. Oh, and Jack?"

"Yes?"

"I'm looking forward to your parade. If I'm not on duty that day, I'll be marching. Bye." She hangs up and I stare at the phone for a few seconds.

Dangerous driving. It sounds like they're saying that Shawn made an illegal U-turn or something like that instead of deliberately swerving into someone on a bike and almost killing him.

Seems obvious that driving a two-ton truck into a bike is dangerous. So obvious that the charge should be more serious, like attempted murder. At the very least, it should be causing bodily harm while driving under the influence of extreme intolerant stupidity.

twenty-four

"It does sound like a bogus charge. He probably won't even get jail time. And I bet Adrian just gets off." Ryan looks disgusted.

"My mom said that it all has to do with intent. Which no one here can prove without anything less than a full confession. As far as I heard, Shawn is trying to say he swerved to avoid a squirrel or something stupid like that, and Adrian is just playing ignorant, which isn't hard for him, because he is. So, I don't think either Shawn or Adrian is going to confess to anything." Cody pulls himself up out of the pool, shaking his hair so he sprays both of us.

"Cody's mom is a lawyer," Ryan says, just in case I didn't know. Which I didn't. Somehow, Cody just doesn't seem like a lawyer's kid.

"A squirrel? Are you kidding me? Everyone knows they

were trying to scare him. That's what you heard, right?" I brush the water out of my eyes.

"That's what I heard, but it's only hearsay. The cops know the truck swerved dangerously and ended up clipping him, but no one can prove that they were aiming for him. Unless Ben can remember more of what happened or Shawn suddenly grows a conscience, there won't be much that anyone can do."

"Benjamin." It comes out louder than I intended, and Cody looks over at me in surprise.

"What?"

"Benjamin. No one calls him *Ben*." I spit the word out as if it tastes like pickles. I hate pickles.

"*I* do," Cody says, grinning at me when I make a face at him. "Anyway, getting Shawn on dangerous driving is better than nothing. And Mom said it's likely dangerous driving causing injury, which is better. Well, better for you, worse for him."

"But he probably won't go to jail?" I can hear the disappointment in my own voice.

"I doubt it. First offense and all."

"First offense?" Ryan snorts. "You were there last year at the dumpsters when that piece of garbage threatened us."

"Which we didn't tell anyone about, so I guess it's the first offense where he got *caught*," Cody corrects himself. "Either way, Mom says he'll likely get probation but could lose his license for quite a while. For Shawn, that's like going to jail. The guy lives in his truck."

"Sounds like a pretty light punishment." I think he should be in jail for at least as long as it takes for Benjamin to get better.

"No one knows what actually happened. So it depends on the lawyer and the judge. It won't be for a while. We'll just have to wait and see. Meantime, at least he's been charged, and everyone knows it. He doesn't have as many people on his side of the fence anymore." Cody dives off the side of the pool, entering the water with barely a ripple before surfacing and taking off full speed, which is how he always swims. He never seems to slow down, never seems to get tired. He was actually offered a swim scholarship to a university but isn't sure he wants to go because he heard that he'll still have to actually do his classwork and keep his marks up. Cody just wants to swim.

"This sucks." It seems inadequate but I've run out of ways to say how much I hate this.

"What does Benjamin think?" Ryan asks. His voice is a bit muffled as he's concentrating on levering his body up and into his chair.

"He's glad they were charged. He's mad at himself for not remembering though. He thinks if he could remember more of what happened that the charge would have been tougher." He had looked so sad that it made my heart hurt. I wish I could wave a magic wand and make this all go away, or better yet, turn everything around so it never happened in the first place.

"Is it too late? What if he remembers later on?"

"That's a good question. I have no idea. Maybe we can get Cody to ask his mom about that." Maybe I should get him to introduce me to her. I have a lot of questions.

"In the meantime, we have enough to focus on. My mom brought a whole pile of artwork home last night that we have to go through and see if we can fit it in with the stuff we already have. We also have to think about the second presentation for the council. Mrs. Lee said that there are already too many people planning to come to stick to the sidewalks."

"They'll still say no. We can't prove that everyone is going to come."

"They can't prove that everyone *isn't* going to come either. And Clare said that lots of people are likely to show up at the last minute without ever even looking at the event page. There could be hundreds of people here."

"Hundreds? Do you really think that's possible?" My voice is somewhere between amazed and horrified.

"If you had asked me six months ago, I would have told you that the idea of a Pride parade in this town would be the farthest thing from possible in the whole freaking universe. And now we're less than two weeks away, and it looks like all kinds of people are going to come. Literally anything is possible these days."

"Maybe you're right. I would never have thought I'd be in the middle of this."

"In the middle? Are you kidding, Jack? You're right at the front of it. The big boss-man. The rest of us are just following your lead. Except right now I can't follow you because I have to go home." He gives me a quick salute and heads over to the change room.

I sit on the edge of the pool and look at the water. They'll be in here cleaning up any minute now, but for this moment I'm alone.

It means a lot that Ryan left me here beside the water. That he didn't wait the way he usually does to make sure that I'm safely out of the community center before leaving me on my own. That he obviously trusts me now and believes that I'm doing okay and understands that I don't want to use large bodies of water for anything but places to think and swim.

I am okay. I keep telling Matthew that, but he won't cancel my sessions until he decides he fully believes me. Which he obviously doesn't. But Ryan does. And Benjamin. Even Cody, who is starting to turn into something resembling a really weird friend.

And I think my mother might have started to believe me too. She's been amazing recently. She had Ryan's mom over last night and the two of them made rainbow armbands for the security guys to wear. I thought it was crazy to think that all those tough guys would wear them, until I found out that it was Cody's idea in the first place. Like I said, weird.

I think Mom's still worried about the distant future, though, and is scared that I'm not going to make it into her idea of heaven. That I'll be turned away at the pearly gates when they find out I spent my life being attracted to guys. But she seems to be getting closer to understanding the idea that while I'm down here on earth, I'm going to find love and happiness in my own way.

I'll always have a different heaven from hers. In her heaven, everyone starts fresh, reborn into something better than before. Blind men can see, and the lame can walk…and I would guess the gays become "straight" if they make it that far. In other words, everyone becomes the same. Walking, talking, and flying. I guess because they're all white-clad angels with wings.

In my heaven, it doesn't matter what you wear or what you can do. No one cares who you want to love or spend time with. Everyone is accepted for exactly who he or she is and no one even thinks of being anything but kind.

It is all about kindness when you get right down to it, whether you're in some version of the afterlife or still living this one. It's the only thing that matters. If everyone just decides to treat everyone else with kindness, it all goes away. Intolerance, disrespect, racism, homophobia, misogyny, bullying, and all the other horrible words we've had to invent just to find a way to label the endless crap people seem to feel the need to throw at each other…all wiped out by one simple command. Be kind.

It's just so simple that I can't understand why everything is always so complicated.

twenty-five

I'm standing on the grass beside Ryan, watching the two cars pull over to the curb and park. I can feel a smile stretching across my face as I wait to see the people who showed me that there is a whole world out there different from the one I've been living in my entire life. It seems like it just happened thirty seconds ago, but it's been almost a full year now since Comic Con. Since the very first time I met people who looked at me like they thought I was someone interesting and worth knowing, not just some weird freak who hangs out by the river and has crushes on boys.

I met Caleb on the first day of the festival. He was the first gay person I had ever talked to in my life. I couldn't believe how incredible that felt. He was so nice to me, and we talked for what felt like hours. He told me all about different support networks that help people like me. He talked about his friends and some of his own experiences. And on top of everything else, he was dressed as Wonder Woman, which was so cool that I almost couldn't stand it. I have to admit, I was a little disappointed when he told me that he only did the dressing up deal for Comic Con and that he liked to alternate between male and female characters just to keep things interesting. Even though meeting someone else who's gay was the most amazing moment of my life to that point, I had still kind of hoped that his sexy skirt and made-up eyes were more than just part of a character he was pretending to be for a day.

But then there was Lucas.

The first time I laid eyes on him, I literally could not look away. Caleb had invited me to meet his friends, and I was sitting in the eating area trying to have lunch while praying that I wouldn't do anything embarrassing or stupid. But I didn't have to worry because everyone was incredibly friendly and accepting. Some of them were doing the cosplay thing and others were wearing cool, colorful clothes that didn't really represent any particular character other than themselves, and one or two people were dressed almost as casually boring as I was.

Oh, but Lucas outshone them all. Tall, muscular, and gorgeous. Dressed as Emma Frost and chowing down on french fries while daintily wiping his lips every few seconds so his silver lipstick didn't smear. His eyes sparkled with glittery shadow that looked like it was made out of crushed diamonds or something, and he had the longest lashes I'd ever seen other than on a screen. His hair was a long sweep of snow-white that he kept flinging back dramatically from his face when he wanted to punctuate something he was saying. Everyone else at the table, including the people in full character dress, paled by comparison, even though there was no color in his costume other than silver and white. Since I had completely chickened out in the costume department, I felt as drab as a plain brown caterpillar staring at some iridescent butterfly. But I didn't really mind because I got the feeling that everyone else at the table felt exactly the same way when Lucas was around, and that they all liked him so much that no one really cared.

I desperately wanted to talk to him and find out if this was just a costume like Caleb's or if it was actually part of who he was. I sat there for what seemed like forever, tongue-tied and desperately trying to find a way to ask a complete stranger something so personal. I had just come up with a brilliant opening line, when Cody, Ryan, and a couple of girls they'd hooked up with crashed my party. The minute they arrived on the scene, I felt like I was back in the Thompson Mills High cafeteria again, and I could actually feel myself shrinking down into my seat.

The girl standing with Ryan was dressed as Rogue from the X-Men, which looked kind of cool with Ryan's Wolverine costume. I looked over at his perfect makeup job. I wonder if he told her I did it for him. Cody was dressed as Captain America and had been spending most of the weekend strutting around like he thought he actually had super powers. Although, he wasn't looking so super standing at a table full of people who seemed to make him remarkably uncomfortable. The thought made me happy and I grinned at him, but he didn't smile back.

Lucas reached over all of a sudden and pulled Rogue over to his side and down onto the white sequined leggings that clung to his muscular legs. The girl giggled as she landed and started helping herself to his fries.

I still remember the look on Ryan's face when she called him over to the table and introduced him to her *brother*, Lucas.

Ryan started acting all weird and macho, which was funny seeing as he was trying to impress a guy in sequins. I'm not sure how impressed Lucas was with the guy who was trying to score with his baby sister, Clare. He held onto the handshake long enough to make Ryan wince. That made me smile from the inside out.

After lunch, Ryan asked me to come with him to check out the rest of the presentations, which was basically pathetic seeing as it was obvious he was trying to spend as much time as possible alone with Clare. I would definitely have cramped his style if I were hanging around. Babysitting 101. I said no and ended up having the best day of my life. Well, the best "before Benjamin" day of my life.

"Jack! I'm so happy to see you in person!" Clare interrupts my little trip down to memory land as she flies across the grass and grabs me into a hug. I hug her back, glancing over her shoulder at Ryan who is looking at her with a besotted smile on his face. She leans back and gives me a kiss on the cheek, then goes over and plops herself down in Ryan's lap.

"Hello there, gorgeous!" Lucas sashays over to me on three-inch stilettos that look like they're going to snap in half any second. Where did he find shoes like that for feet like his?

There's nothing small about Lucas. He's at least six one and his feet have to be size eleven.

"Hi Lucas," I say, my voice muffled into oblivion as he grabs me in a bear hug. He also leans back and gives me a kiss but his is right on the mouth. It's the first time I've been kissed on the lips by a guy. Not the guy I was aiming for, but I grin at him anyway.

"This is my friend, Jackson, the amazing organizer of the grand event," he says, pulling another man I haven't met before toward me by the arm. "Jackson, this is my fiancé, Jamal. I do love saying that!"

"I'm really happy to meet you. Clare and Lucas talk about you a lot." Jamal reaches over to shake my hand. He's tall, but a bit shorter than Lucas. Bigger though, muscles over muscles in a way Cody would envy. He's wearing jeans and a T-shirt, which will make him fit in Thompson Mills just fine. He's also Black, which will make him stand out from the crowd of mostly white faces here.

"Heya, kid!" Caleb steps up with a giant grin and does the handshake thing also. I squeeze his hand tightly for a second before letting go.

"It's awesome to see all of you. I can't believe you're all actually here. I can't believe the parade is the day after tomorrow!" I'm so glad there are reinforcements. Now that the day is almost here, I'm walking around in a haze of panic.

It'll be even better when Benjamin gets home too.

"We're glad to be here. And everyone else from Bainesville will be thrilled. We're expecting quite a crowd," Lucas says.

"I know. The numbers online are crazy. It's up over a hundred. It's like some kind of dream sequence or something," I tell him. One hundred and six, as of last count.

"Oh, it's going to be much bigger than that. I imagine there are lots of people who will arrive without bothering with social media. I never bother with it."

"Yes, you do, Lucas!" Clare says.

"Well, I seldom use it then. It's so…yesterday."

"Which I'm pretty sure is the last time you used it!" Clare laughs. "So, are they closing the road?" she asks from her perch on Ryan's lap. He smiles at her as if she just said something brilliant. What a sap.

"Not yet. Mr. Greenman slash Mayor said we'll take a wait-and-see approach. He doesn't believe the numbers."

"He's wishing that no one will come. He's terrified that the media will have something to report," Ryan says, nuzzling his nose against Clare's arm while she ruffles his red hair. Seriously sappy.

Man, I wish Benjamin was here right now. Not that we're at the sappy lap-sitting stage or anything, but still…

"They'll have lots to report. This is going to be fabulous. Better than." Lucas heads over to the car and grabs a giant suitcase. I look over to where he's standing in his pretty green skirt and matching high-heeled shoes with a big black bag tucked under one arm like a football. I know that most people around here would just about pass out if they saw him coming their way, but to me he just looks like Lucas. Big, bold, and sure of who he is. When I grow up, I want to be exactly like him.

"Where are we bunking?" he asks, marching up the front pathway toward the house.

"Oh, you and Jamal are staying here. Caleb and Clare are staying at Ryan's." Lucas stops, sets the bag down, and turns around slowly, giving Ryan the stink eye.

"And exactly *where* is it that Clare is staying at Ryan's?" he asks, staring Ryan down.

"She is staying in the guest room, beside my parents' room, and at the other end of the hall from mine. Caleb is sleeping in the room between my parents' and mine," Ryan says quickly as Clare laughs.

"That better be true," Lucas says.

"It is true. You haven't met my mother. You won't be worried once you do. Which you will tonight at dinner, because she's having everyone over. Jack's mom has to work until six, so Mom figured we'd all eat at our place."

"Oh, we don't want to put your mother out either. Isn't there a restaurant in town? I'll treat." Lucas reaches for his purse.

"No, believe me, you don't want to have supper at the Supe. My mom is more than happy to have everyone. My dad does most of the cooking anyway. He's kind of an amateur chef."

"Sounds wonderful. We'll get settled here and head on over." Lucas heads back up the front walk, strutting along with the bag as if it weighs nothing. Jamal follows behind with a small carry-on-sized bag.

He grins at me. "I travel light. It balances us out a bit."

"Makes sense. I'm just going to say good-bye to these guys

and then I'll be in to show you your room." He nods and follows Lucas. I turn to Ryan.

"What time should we be there?"

"Anytime you want. Mom's already home so there'll be food starting any time. Are you okay?" He looks up toward the house, where Lucas is just arriving at the door. We had debated the best way to find beds for everyone. At first, I wasn't sure that introducing my mother to Lucas would be the best start to the next phase of her LGBTQ+ education. But we only have one extra bedroom and Ryan has two, so practicality won the day.

Besides, Lucas is awesome. If anyone can win my mom over, he can.

"Yeah. I'm great," I tell him, waving as I head up the walkway and into the house with Lucas and Jamal.

"So, this is the spare room. It's not much, but Mom changed the sheets on the bed for you and everything." Lucas grins at me as he and Jamal look through the doorway at the double bed and small dresser surrounded by drab gray walls. I follow their gaze and wince. I should have bought some posters and tacked them up or something. This place is awful.

"It's perfect. Are you sure you're okay with this? With your mom?" Lucas says. He knows all about my mom and her struggles with accepting me.

"Yes. She was pretty cool when I explained that you only need one bed. At least she pretended to be. Besides, she's got to learn some time, right?" Lucas looks at me, arms folded, one green-pointed toe tapping.

"Well, maybe she doesn't have to learn everything in one

weekend. Having an engaged couple here might be enough. You told Clare that she wouldn't be here when we arrived, so I just came as I am, but I brought some reverse drag outfits and I have lots of makeup remover on hand if you think it would help. I can keep all of this out of sight." He does a sweeping gesture down his body with both hands and then looks over at his fiancé. "Jamal already passes, I think."

I think about it for a few seconds. My mom is really trying to get her head around all of this. She's been helping get ready for the parade, even though she can't come because she's working. She works six days a week, which I'm pretty sure is against some kind of labor law. She's tired all of the time but is still making an effort. *Is* it too much to expect her to handle seeing Lucas in a dress and makeup? Should I ask him to switch it up? He's standing there looking awesome but willing to change it all to make life easier for me. I shake my head.

"No. I'm not going to ask you to hide who you are. That's what this is all about, isn't it? Coming out into the light. Not hiding anymore."

"All right then. I have to change."

"I just said you don't have to change." I look at him in confusion. He and Jamal both laugh.

"I can't wear this old thing to dinner," Lucas says. "I've been sitting in it for hours. I need to make a good first impression." He grabs the big black bag and starts pulling things out of it. Clothes and shoes. Hats and wigs. A jacket in case it suddenly turns cold in June. It all starts piling up on the bed until I can't see the blanket anymore. He's like a really big version of Mary Poppins and her magic bag. He stops for a moment and considers me.

"This *is* about not hiding anymore. Anytime you're ready, I'm always willing to share." He sweeps a hand across the pile on the bed. I look at it for a few seconds and nod slowly.

"That would be great. I think I'd need some help figuring out what would suit me. This is like a pop-up store."

"This is only the half of it," Lucas says, laughing.

Jamal shakes his head, smiling at Lucas in a way that melts my heart. "The half of it? I would say it's more like the tenth or twelfth of it."

"Guilty as charged." Lucas holds out his arms toward Jamal as though he's expecting handcuffs.

"I think I'll let you get settled. I have to do a few things. We'll head over to Ryan's when you're ready."

"I hope you're not in a hurry." Jamal laughs, looking at Lucas again with an expression that I can only dream of seeing in someone's eyes someday.

Someone who's going to be here tomorrow. I can't wait. I know people always say that, but I actually feel like I *can't*. Like my head might explode at the thought that he's still twenty-four hours away from coming home. I want to hop into Caleb's car and drive until I see Benjamin's face live and in person again.

Of course, I don't have my license, so that probably wouldn't be a very good idea. There's already been enough dangerous driving around here.

twenty-six

"Your friends are lovely," Mom says to me, smiling as she stirs up the batter for pancakes. "I really enjoyed dinner last night. Such lively conversations!"

Lively might be understating it. Lucas took center stage for the evening, telling stories that a year ago would have made my mother pass out on the floor in horror. He's so funny and full of energy that everyone, including my mom, was laughing so hard that they practically spit the awesome meal that Mr. Malloy cooked back out onto the table a few times.

"Are they both still sleeping? Jamal is such a nice man. So serious. Quite the opposite of his…partner? Is that the right word?"

"Partner's fine. Lucas mostly likes *fiancé* though."

"Oh, right, they're getting married." She takes a deep breath and turns back to her pancakes. She stirs and flips for a while then turns back to me. "Do you think about getting married some day?"

I look at her. She's asked me this before, but I know she always meant "do you think you're going to marry a woman some day?" But I don't think that's what she's asking now. I take a deep breath.

"I hope so."

She nods. "What about children? I've always wanted to be an *abuelita*." She smiles a little sadly. I never thought about that part of it. That she might have been worried that my being gay meant that she'll never be a grandma.

"I like kids. I hope to have them someday."

"But how?"

"There are different options. Lucas and Jamal want to use a surrogate. A woman who will actually carry one or both of their biological kids," I add just on the off chance she doesn't know what it is. "There's also adoption. It will depend on who I marry and what we both decide, I guess." She nods and then comes over to give me a kiss on the cheek before turning back to breakfast. She stirs the pancake batter for a few seconds and then turns to look at me.

"Lucas is very beautiful. He seems so comfortable in his lovely clothes. I think it is very nice that he can dress the way he feels. *Everyone* should be able to do that." She reaches over and strokes my cheek, smiling a little. My eyes suddenly fill up with tears, and I have to sniff loudly to keep them in check.

"*Buenos días*, Pedersens!" Lucas sings out as he strides into the room, saving me from dissolving into a snotty mess. He clicks across the linoleum in his signature stilettos in hot pink to match his—I want to say *shorts*, but he probably has some other fashion label for them. The pink is set off by a deep-blue, tight-fitting T-shirt.

"*Buenos días!* You look lovely today, Lucas," Mom says, affection obvious in her voice. "Those look like hot pants from the seventies."

"Right you are, Mrs. P. You know your vintage fashion. Can I help with breakfast?"

"Sure, why don't you help Jack set the table? Not that he offered," Mom answers, giving me a mock stern look. I grin at her and lead the way to the dish cupboard, where I hand plates and cups to Lucas.

"Good morning, everyone," Jamal says quietly as he comes into the room. "What can I do to help?"

"Such polite boys. You have a few things to learn from these two," Mom says to me just as Lucas goes over and gives Jamal a good morning kiss. Right in front of my mother. I glance at her to see her reaction. All she does is smile.

She's right. I do have a lot to learn from these two. Maybe I should start with that pop-up store in the bedroom.

Mrs. Lee gave us the day off to get things ready. We'll be using the arena as the start point tomorrow. It's only a block away from Main Street. It has a huge parking lot and an adjoining field where cars can be parked in case we actually do get a large crowd. I'm still not convinced it's going to happen that way, but at this point, I don't care. I know there are some people coming from Bainesville, and Ryan and Benjamin both say they have friends coming too. Ten people, twenty, or even one hundred and six…anything would be just fine with me.

Benjamin. Looks like I might not see him until the parade tomorrow. He has a doctor's appointment late this afternoon that he wasn't able to change, so his dad is driving him up tomorrow morning instead of today. That sucks in every possible way, but there's nothing I can do about it except work so hard today that I don't notice the time crawling by.

After we finish eating and cleaning up, Jamal drives me over to the school to pick up the materials we made and take them over to the arena. On the way, we stop and pick up Caleb at Ryan's house. Ryan, Clare, and Lucas are staying there to work on Lucas's speech for the rally and to download the music we're going to use before meeting us at the arena.

The rally is a chance for people to tell their own stories and to share information. Lucas and Caleb are going to speak for sure, along with anyone else who wants to step up to the mic. Lucas wants me to talk because this whole thing was my idea, but I'm really not a speech-maker. Addressing the council and our make-shift Rainbow Club was enough public speaking to last me a lifetime. I don't want to talk about myself in public. Everyone already knows more than enough about me.

Ryan agrees with Lucas, but I think Benjamin is the one who should speak. Everyone would listen to that beautiful voice. But he told me it would be enough effort just to be there and participate and that he'd rather listen to me. He's been trying to persuade me into it for days, and if he tries again, he'll probably succeed because I have a really hard time saying no to those eyes. So, I hope he doesn't try. I really just want to march.

Jamal and I walk down the hallway, bringing on the usual stares and whispers. It takes a few seconds for me to realize that the eyes aren't focused on me today. They're staring at the tall, gorgeous man beside me who definitely stands out in the sea of white faces that flows down the halls of TMHS. I think that Henry, the man Benjamin noticed who owns the gas station, has a son who goes here, but besides him, this is probably the least diverse school in the country. I have no idea why it's so homogenous, but it doesn't really help with the whole "learning how to accept differences" thing when there aren't any visible "differences" floating around.

Jamal seems cheerfully oblivious as we walk down to the art room. All of the work done by our makeshift Rainbow Club is neatly piled on the teacher's desk, so we take it and put it carefully into big garbage bags to carry out to the car. As we start to leave the room, I stand and look at Benjamin's rainbow.

"I think we should bring it," I say to Jamal.

"Pardon?"

"The stone rainbow. It's Benjamin's art project. It's kind of what started this whole thing. I think we can figure out a way to attach something to it, so it can be carried tomorrow." Jamal looks at it speculatively and then goes over and lifts it slightly.

"It's only plywood so it isn't that heavy, even with all of the stones on it." He shakes it a little. "They seem pretty secure as well. I can attach a couple of strong dowels without damaging it and find a couple of folks to carry it."

"That would be great."

We load the garbage bags into the car and then come back for the rainbow, carefully lifting it off the shelf and carrying it down the hall like a mini-parade procession just for TMHS. This would be a good time for Shawn to show up and try to intimidate me. Between Jamal and my big pile of colored stones, he wouldn't stand a chance.

Mrs. Lee follows us out to the car.

"I'll drop the prefab flags off in the morning. They just came in last night. Cutting it close. I assume you know Benjamin isn't coming until tomorrow?" She looks at me. I try a smile, but it doesn't quite work.

"Yes, he told me. At least he's coming."

"He is, and he's determined to try walking the route. He's using a cane right now, as you likely know, but he can't go far very comfortably. We might have to gang up on him and persuade him to use a wheelchair for at least part of the walk. His dad is going to bring it along. I imagine that will be a bit of a fight." She smiles.

"I'll do what I can, but I'm not sure he'll listen to me," I tell her.

"Oh, you'd be surprised!" she says, with a look in her eyes that makes me smile flat out.

"Thanks for your help with all of this, Mrs. Lee."

"No, Jackson. I thank you. I know you did this in great part for Benjamin. It has just lifted him up and made him quite fiercely determined to get better so that he can be here.

He was so depressed after the accident that I was worried about his recovery."

"Really? He always seems so strong and sure of himself."
Depressed? Benjamin?

"He's a pretty good actor. He uses it as a bit of a shield against things that try to bring him down. It doesn't always work. You'll find that out as you get to know him better."

As I get to know him better. Not *if.* Like she thinks I'm going to be around for a while.

"I look forward to it."

"And I'm looking forward to tomorrow. Good luck with the rest of the preparations. I'll see you at noon at the arena to help with the last-minute things." She turns and heads back into the school.

Lucas, Caleb, and Clare meet us in the parking lot of the arena, and we all unload the car, taking everything inside. We spend the next couple of hours stapling posters and banners onto thin dowels that were donated by the local hardware store, which is surprising seeing as the owner is on the town council and wasn't exactly supportive at either meeting. He wasn't unsupportive either. Just conspicuously silent. But he's helping now, so it's all good. Jamal has gone over to the store to see if he's willing to donate one more set of dowels strong enough to hold up the stone rainbow without breaking.

We have a giant banner made up of a collage of kids' artwork from Ryan's mom's school. On it is every possible size, shape, and color of rainbow. There are some super cute pictures of rainbows wearing crowns, with our slogan "Rainbows Reign" on them. There's even one picture of a bunch of teeny tiny rainbows falling from a cloud, made by someone who obviously decided to change the spelling of reign.

We have large posters that just say *Pride*, others that show hearts with *Love Wins* on them. Not as original as rainbows raining from the clouds, but seeing as this whole event is a first in this town, everything is going to seem new and different to anyone who takes the time to watch us. There are about fifty flags in the box Mrs. Lee gave us, already on sticks and ready to fly in the breeze tomorrow. We also have around twenty rainbow-colored scepters that Sarah and Nancy designed.

It's supposed to be a nice day, sunny and warm but not too hot. The mayor will be disappointed.

The local police are on standby but not officially assigned to help us, other than to assess the numbers at 1:30, a half hour before start time, and decide whether or not to barricade Main Street for a few minutes to let us actually walk properly. Other than that, we have a dozen armbands for Cody's security crew, who I'm still hoping won't have anything to do but walk around looking terrifying.

Word spread quickly about Shawn being charged. I don't know what that's doing to public opinion about the parade and whether or not it will discourage the local hate society from coming out and making life difficult for us tomorrow. The negative comments are still popping up daily online, and I'm still deleting them.

It would be nice if you could do that to the actual people… just delete their negative comments and go about your business as if nothing had happened. Or better yet, delete the whole person—I'd like to do that to Shawn.

Still no trial date. Cody said his mom thinks it could be up to a year, or even longer. By then, most people will have forgotten what he did. Shawn, being a boy of very little brain, will likely have no idea what the lawyers are talking about by then. It seems like a weak system when everyone has to wait that long for something resembling justice.

"Jack! Wake up!" I feel a finger in my ribs, which makes me jump and drop the flag I'd been standing here staring at.

"Ow! Ryan, you need to cut your fingernails or, even better, don't poke me!"

"Clare has asked you twice where you want the banner to go now that it's ready."

I look over to where she's standing with the rolled-up banner in her hands. She waves at me cheerfully.

"Anywhere you can find a spot is fine," I call over to her.

"Are you okay?" Ryan asks.

"Yeah. Just taking a mental break for two seconds."

"It's going great. We're pretty much ready. Just get a good sleep tonight and it'll be tomorrow before you know it."

"Don't remind me! I feel like the whole town is watching and expecting me to screw this up."

"That's all in your mind. It isn't the whole town at all. Half, maybe three quarters, tops." Ryan grins as Lucas comes up behind him and bops him on the head with a rolled-up poster.

"That is not helpful, Red!" he says, hitting him again. I look at Ryan's face to get his reaction. He hates being called Red.

"Just trying to keep it real, Luke," Ryan says, using the name that Lucas hates being called.

"Call me that again and I won't be using paper."

"You'd threaten a poor little kid in a wheelchair?" Ryan asks, putting a pathetic look on his face. Lucas laughs.

"You bet! I believe in equality." He heads off to help Clare organize the rest of the flags, laying them all out on a table so they're easy to grab tomorrow.

I look at my phone. Less than twenty-four hours now.

Everyone is so proud of me for standing up for Pride.

I really hope I don't fall on my face.

twenty-seven

I toss and turn all night, dreaming about gargoyles that eat rainbows and white pickup trucks that transform into hulking homophobes who chase everyone in the parade, stomping on the innocent like we're in some kind of dystopian YA movie. I wake up several times in a cold sweat, finally giving up on sleep at 5:00 a.m.

I get up and take a shower, standing under the hot stream for as long as I can stand it, hoping that it might soak away the panic that started with my dreams and is continuing into the reality of what this day is about to bring. It doesn't work, so I dry off and go turn on my tablet, trying to find something to watch and distract me for a while until it's late enough to actually start the day.

A message icon jumps out at me, and I click on it. It's a video message with the best possible image I could see at five in the morning...or any other time for that matter.

"Good morning. I wanted to actually call, but I wasn't sure when you'd be up so I thought this way I wouldn't wake you accidentally. Although my guess is that you didn't sleep much. I wouldn't if I were you! Just wanted to say I'm heading your way soon and I can't wait. The parade is going to be awesome. You are totally awesome. It's going to be a great day and you should feel proud, which fits nicely with the theme, I guess! Oh, and I really think you should make a speech at the rally. Bye!"

Benjamin grins widely at me from the screen as he blows a kiss. Without thinking, I reach out my hand to catch it.

I'm really glad no one was here to see that.

I thought the one advantage—the only one—of his coming so late was that he wouldn't have time to try to persuade me to talk at the rally. But he just asked me so nicely, with a kiss and everything!

Deep down...well, not so deep, pretty much right there at the surface, I know he's right. I started this. I have to take it all the way. Which means I can use all of this nice extra time this morning to figure out what the hell I'm going to say.

Trying to come up with brilliant words when you spent most of the night having hallucinatory dreams takes up more time than you'd think. The morning speeds by so quickly that Mom is at the door telling me that my ride is here before I even make it out of my room to grab breakfast.

I find Lucas and Jamal standing in the kitchen with my mother. Lucas is literally decked out in every color of the rainbow, starting with the red crown on his yellow wigged head, down to the bright-pink ruffled shirt tucked into a gorgeous purple-and-blue striped skirt that looks like it would swirl beautifully if he decided to dance, which he might do with those sparkling turquoise shoes on his feet. Jamal is wearing a tie-dyed, multi-colored T-shirt with jeans and red running shoes. Pretty out there for him.

I'm suddenly really conscious of my plain green T-shirt and denim jeans. I didn't even think about my clothes and forgot I'd told Lucas I was going to check out his supplies.

"Are you ready?" Lucas asks, looking me up and down with a face that says he clearly doesn't think I'm anywhere close.

"I guess so," I tell him, disappointed in myself. This is not how I want to look today of all days. I actually forgot that I'm supposed to be part of the rainbow. Maybe Benjamin will bring his blanket and I can tie it around my neck like a superhero cape.

"Good luck, honey. I love you. And I'm proud of you," Mom says, a bit teary eyed. She hands me a granola bar like she used to when I was in grade school and gives me a kiss.

"Thanks, Mom. You know what? I'm proud of you too," I say quickly and then run down the front steps to the car while she wipes her eyes.

We get to the arena at around noon, two hours before the parade is due to start. There are already at least twenty cars in the parking lot and a small crowd of people milling around, talking and laughing.

"Early birds," Lucas says. "Looks like at least fifty. And that's just the beginning."

I don't recognize anyone. I didn't expect to. I also didn't expect so many people here already.

As we walk over to the building, Lucas chats to everyone he passes. I can't tell if he knows the people he's talking to or not. That sort of thing doesn't matter to him. He'll talk to anyone he meets whether they want him to or not.

Clare, Ryan, Caleb, Mrs. Malloy, and Mrs. Lee are inside. Mr. Malloy is there too, working on the portable sound system that we're going to use. I head over to talk to him for a few seconds, so he can show me how it works. If I have to talk today, I want to at least have something that will project my voice.

"Hi! Are you all set?" Mrs. Malloy asks when I finish with her husband and head over to where they're laying out posters.

"Sure...I guess." My voice sounds as uncertain as I feel. She smiles and ruffles my hair. Lucas walks over and looks at me critically.

"I disagree. I didn't want to say anything in front of your lovely mama, but seriously, what is all this?" He sweeps his hand up and down in front of me.

"This is me," I say.

"Is it really?" he asks. "I don't think so. It's like you're trying to hide in plain sight. Come with me." He grabs my hand and leads me over to the other side of the room before I have a chance to protest. He marches me up to a table that is holding most of the clothes and makeup that used to be lying across the bed at home. *How did he pack it up so fast?*

"Come, come. We have time. Everything is ready, and people are just starting to arrive. We need to give you some color. The theme is rainbows and you look like a blade of grass."

"I don't…" I'm not sure how I was planning to finish that sentence, but Lucas doesn't give me a chance to find out.

"I know you're not ready to go full-on Lucas yet. But a little color on those cheeks and some enhancing of your beautiful eyes. Some shaping of the lips. A bit of help controlling those gorgeous curls with some color added here and there." He's working while he talks. I seem to have lost control of my free will because I just stand there letting him work. I can't believe I'm right here in public, having makeup put on me. I've only ever worn it in my bedroom at home, at night after my mom goes to bed. It feels terrifying and wonderful at the same time.

"There!" he says, holding a mirror up to my face. Was that in the suitcase too? I make myself look.

"Oh."

"Yes, *oh*. You are lovely," he tells me. I'm not sure if I'm lovely or not, but it's not bad. I'm pretty good at putting on makeup, but Lucas is definitely a pro. It's obviously there but somehow subtle at the same time. My hair looks as curly as usual, but it shines a little, and all the frizz seems tamer. Less like a Brillo pad and more like actual hair that looks soft enough to touch. There are shimmers of color in the blackness…sparkling streaks of bright green and yellow, with some purple in there too. I'm not sure how he got it in there, but I hope it isn't paint or something. My eyes look bigger and brighter, but you can't immediately tell why. They're sparkling too, and I lean closer to see. My lids are covered in gold eye shadow that glistens like a million tiny sequins made their way into the mix. My lashes are pitch-black and thicker than usual, curling upward, making my eyes pop out from my face. A face that looks delicately flushed but not the fire-engine red I manage to create every time I get embarrassed. Maybe the artificial color will cover the natural flaring up when I have to stand at the microphone and try to remember what I wrote in a half-asleep stupor this morning.

It's better than not bad. It's good. Maybe even lovely.

"Thanks," I say inadequately. There should be more said, but I'm still staring at myself in something close to awe. I look down at as much as I can see of the rest of me. The dull green is even duller now compared to my face.

"There's more. Here." I tear my eyes away from myself as he hands me a filmy piece of fabric that floats as it comes toward me. It takes a second to realize that it's a shirt, long and silky, with an intricate pattern blending so many colors together that I can't see them all. It's just an overall impression of color, like an abstract painting that you wear on your back.

"Just slip it over your T-shirt and let it flow," Lucas says, helping me put it on. It hangs down to my knees, covering up most of my drabness, making me feel like some kind of psyche-delic butterfly when I walk away with it floating out behind me.

"I love it!" I tell him, and he grins as he holds out one last thing.

"One more thing to finish the look." He hands me a pale yellowish-gold bundle, and for a split second I wonder if he somehow managed to save my mother's skirt from wherever Ryan hid it that day at the river. It takes another second to realize that it's actually a pair of soft leggings. They look like they're his, which means they're long enough for his endless legs.

"I know they're long, but that will help hide those sneakers. They've seen better days. Just pull them right down over the heel and don't worry about them. I have lots more where those came from."

I hesitate for a moment but then run into the bathroom and strip off my jeans. I pull on the stretchy fabric. The leggings slide up my legs like a second skin that is loose enough to make room for a few extra calories but doesn't sag so much that it looks weird. I put my shoes back on and then pull the extra length down over the heels, which looks much cooler in reality than it did in my mind.

I stand and stare in the mirror, trying to see as much of myself as possible. My hair shimmers with subtle color in the dull bathroom light. My shiny gold eyelids make me look exotic. The gorgeous flowing rainbow shirt wraps around me like a multi-colored cloud.

I look good. Better than good.

Maybe *this* is me.

I tear myself away from the mirror and head out into the arena.

"You look great," Clare says as I come up to where she's getting ready to march.

"Thanks," I say a bit self-consciously, resisting the temptation to run over to Lucas so I can grab his mirror and take another look.

"Hey, Jack? You'd better get out here," Ryan calls to me from the doorway. I run across the room, thinking some catastrophe has happened. I get to the door and Ryan takes a quick glance at me. "Nice shirt. You look like a butterfly or something." He seems oblivious to the rest of me. I can't decide if that's good or bad.

"Thanks. I think."

"Better than an ugly caterpillar." He laughs, and I look at him in surprise. I didn't think he'd remember. Once upon a time I told him that I wished I could be a caterpillar so that I could just disappear for a while into a nice safe cocoon. Then I could grow a couple of wings so I could fly far away from here where no one would ever find me, and I could be as beautiful as I want to be because no one cares if a butterfly is a boy or a girl. It's just a pretty part of nature that everyone accepts.

At the time, I'm pretty sure he thought I was nuts. I think we've both come a long way since then. Ryan doesn't want to be my babysitter anymore, and I don't want to be a caterpillar anymore. He's figured out how to be my friend, and I've apparently gone straight to butterfly.

I grin at him but then just stop and stare, mesmerized by the scene in front of us. Everywhere I look, there are cars and people. The parking lot is completely full, and the field beyond it is rapidly filling up. People are wandering around everywhere, some of them with their own flags and posters, others dressed in crazy costumes. It's like a giant field of colorful wildflowers that suddenly sprouted legs and started to move. Everyone looks happy and excited.

"There must be at least three hundred people, maybe more," Ryan says. "Mrs. Lee has gone over to talk to the mayor and the police about getting the road closed."

I just nod, too amazed to find a single word. That should be helpful during the rally.

"Told you." Lucas comes up behind me, putting both hands on my shoulders.

"It's going to be so awesome, Jack," Clare says, wrapping her arm around my waist.

"Any room for me in this group hug?" Benjamin walks up slowly, leaning on his cane, a huge grin on his face. I was so busy staring at the crowd that I didn't see him coming.

"Come on in! You can have my spot. I'm Lucas, by the way. Not that you're interested in me at the moment!" Lucas says, laughing as he and Clare both step away from me. I can feel my pink cheeks heating up as Benjamin comes over and wraps one arm around me, still balancing on his cane with the other.

"I missed you," he says into my ear.

"Me too," I say back, holding on for a few seconds. He steps back carefully, looking me over. I'm feeling so nervous and self-conscious that I'm sweating. Any minute now my face is going to start melting and drip down onto my shirt, blending in with the rest of the colors.

"You look gorgeous. I feel underdressed," he says. He's wearing a bright blue T-shirt with a rainbow and Kermit the Frog printed across the front and green pants a shade brighter than the frog.

"You look pretty rainbow themed," I tell him. He smiles and points to his cane.

"Check this out. My mom got it." I look at it and realize that it's covered with tiny rainbows and clouds that remind me of the raining rainbows painting that came from the little kid at Ryan's mom's school.

"And his dad got this," Mr. Lee says as he walks up to us, pushing a wheelchair. Benjamin makes a face.

"I don't need that, Dad."

"Well, I just might. These heels might not do well on these rural streets," Lucas says. "We'll just decorate it up and bring it along in case." He smiles at Benjamin, who shakes his head at the obvious ploy but mouths "thanks" anyway.

"Fine, whatever works. Happy now, Dad?"

"Good enough for me. I'm going to go wait for your mother. See you at the march."

The march. I suppose that technically this is a march, not a parade because we aren't doing floats or entertainment. But we're saying it's a parade anyway, because this is our day and we can call it whatever we want.

"Oh, hey—there they are!" Ryan shouts. I look over to where he's pointing. There's a group of about fifteen or twenty wheelchairs heading our way. "I wasn't expecting that many people. This is awesome! Talk to you later." He heads off to join them, navigating his way expertly through the crowd.

"Look at him go. I never got my crappy wheelchair moving that fast," Benjamin says.

"Ryan is really strong. You should see him swim," I tell him.

"Jack, I've been looking for you. Hello, sweetheart!" Mrs. Lee gives Benjamin a big kiss. Now why didn't I do that?

"Hi, Mom."

"Jackson, Main Street is officially closed as of one minute ago. We're ready!"

I instantly have a total and complete panic reaction. *Look at all of these people! How am I supposed to get them all to listen to me and get in some sort of order? No one is going to pay any attention to me!*

"Jackson?"

"Yes, what?" I look at her distractedly. *So many people!*

"The sound system is set up here and we're ready to start. I'll use my teacher voice to get things going." She smiles, and I take a deep breath as I remember. Right. I'm not doing this part. We decided that Mrs. Lee would get everyone organized and then I would welcome them. I can do that.

Mrs. Lee grabs the mic and announces that the parade is about to begin. The crowd responds to her pretty much the same way the kids at school do. Within a few minutes all the flags and posters are handed out and being held high. Everyone is standing, looking expectant.

"Before we begin, I'd like to introduce the organizer of today's event, Jackson Pedersen!"

Everyone claps, which startles me so much that I almost forget that I'm supposed to talk.

"Thanks for that," I say into the mic. The applause dies down and everyone looks at me.

"My name is Jackson Pedersen. I'm a senior in the high school here in Thompson Mills." The applause starts again, louder this time. Are they clapping for Thompson Mills? They obviously don't understand where they are!

"I want to welcome you all here," I shout into the microphone, trying to make myself heard. "And invite you to join us on this very first Pride parade. If you'll just follow the folks with the banner," I point to Lucas, Caleb, and Clare, "we'll lead the way down Main Street to our rally at the Town Hall. Thanks for coming!"

As I walk over to help hoist the banner, I see Jamal coming toward me with Benjamin's stone rainbow mounted on two thick sticks. He stops in front of me and smiles.

"I thought you'd like to help me with this. You look pretty strong. Also gorgeous, by the way. I recognize Lucas's handiwork, I think."

"Oh, my god, that's awesome!" Benjamin comes over and stares at his artwork. "I wish I could help but I'd probably fall over!"

"No problem. I can do it." As I grab the left side and help Jamal hoist it up, I'm instantly glad the march is a short one. I have a different opinion than Jamal about how heavy this thing is! We turn to move to the head of the line and one of the red stones drops onto the ground. I bend down and pick it up before Benjamin can notice that his project is falling apart. I stare at it for a second, the red paint a sudden sickening reminder of the sight of Benjamin's blood pooling on the rocks at the bottom of the embankment. I shake the image away. It doesn't belong to this day. Today is about the future, not the past. I put the stone in my shirt pocket and stand up.

"If we get any unruly jerks along the way, we can always throw rainbow-colored rocks at them." Lucas laughs as he comes over to give Jamal a kiss on the cheek.

"Not so much. Pretty sure violence of any color is frowned upon."

"I'd have to agree with that." I look over toward the voice. Officer Peabody is standing there in full uniform. "I am here to officially inform you that there will be a police presence today after all. We will be walking beside you, helping to keep the peace. I only wish I could carry a flag!" She smiles as she steps away.

As I watch her walk over to the crowd of people, I spot Sarah Edey and her friends, talking three hundred words a minute and looking excited to be here. I'm not sure, but I think a few other kids from school are here as well. Someone waves from the left side of the crowd, and I'm surprised to see that it's Matthew. I've been so busy recently that I skipped my last couple of sessions with him and I never even told him I was going to be doing this. It's seriously cool that he's here. He's even wearing some kind of crazy looking multi-colored hat and waving a rainbow flag, which is definitely a better look than his usual boring black jeans and white button-up shirt.

Cody is standing over by the edge of the first group of people, and when I look farther, I see the rest of his squad spread out down the line. I don't know if the police will be happy to have an amateur team there or not, but I'm happy to see them. As far as I know, no one has thrown or yelled anything at us, but then again, we haven't actually started walking yet.

So, we do.

We march our way out of the parking lot, across one small field, and straight onto Main Street. I wonder briefly if anyone will be annoyed when they realize they traveled hours to walk for about twenty minutes through our tiny town, but then the thought disappears as people start to chant and sing their way through Thompson Mills, wearing and waving every color of the rainbow as they go.

twenty-eight

Between making sure I keep my side of the rainbow as high as Jamal's and trying to listen to everyone and watch everything at the same time, I barely notice people looking at us as we march by. I briefly see some curious faces and others that look less than thrilled. I think I might have heard the word *fag* screamed at me as I walked past, but it was drowned out so quickly I'm not sure. I see Cody out of the corner of my eye as he seems to head toward someone, but I move on before I can tell what he's doing.

There are so many of us that even if somebody wanted to cause trouble, they'd have a hard time. The entire street is filled with people singing and chanting. Ryan and his friends are wheeling along two by two, surrounded, and in some cases being pushed, by incredibly colorful people who could give Lucas a run for his money.

Benjamin is doing great. There are so many people that we're moving really slowly, and he's able to keep up without resorting to the chair. Lucas is having a lot of fun with it though, giving people rides and then having a ride himself to rest his sparkly feet. Every few minutes I look over, and when he sees me do it, he grins with an *I-told-you-so* expression that makes me feel like dancing.

Lots of other people are dancing along the street, so I'd fit right in. This is so much fun! I wasn't expecting that. Everyone is just celebrating being here together. No one seems worried about who might be watching or judging. And that's what this is all about, isn't it?

This is our time. Right here. Right now. And very soon it is going to be my time because Thompson Mills is so small that we're already at the Town Hall.

As we reach the steps, I am surprised to see four council members standing there holding flags.

"Hi, Jack," says the woman who helped me at the meeting. "We just wanted to show our support." The other three all smile and nod. *Mr. Mayor* is conspicuous by his absence.

"Thanks. We appreciate it," I tell her as we walk up to where Mr. Malloy has set up the sound system for the rally. There's already music blasting through the speakers, which keeps people moving, even after they arrive at the bottom of the steps.

It takes a while for everyone to get caught up. Lucas waits a few minutes, smiling happily as he watches the crowd milling around, singing and dancing, and having a blast. He turns to Mr. Malloy and nods, stepping up to the mic as the music dies down.

"Hello, and welcome to the Thompson Mills Pride Parade!" Lucas shouts, ignoring the fact that we told him the mayor expressly asked us not to call it that. The one media reporter who decided to come and cover the event records the name for posterity. Everyone cheers and claps.

"You are all gorgeous!" The cheers get louder and a few people yell out, "So are you!" Lucas laughs and waits a few seconds for the noise to die down a bit before he speaks again. "Today we honor all those who have come before us and have taken a stand against intolerance, discrimination, and violence, and we encourage all of you who do so today and in the future. We are here, and we are proud. I am a proud gay man...who's getting married!" He sings the last word and holds his ring out for the crowd to see. Everyone breaks into crazy applause. He waits a few seconds and starts to speak again. "There are still far too many places in the world where I couldn't be standing here wearing an engagement ring, looking forward to being legally married. Days like this one are important, so that we can keep on spreading the message that love is love." Jamal walks up and puts his arm around Lucas, giving him a kiss that looks like something out of a romantic movie. Everyone cheers, with a bunch of people taking up the chant "love is love."

"Rainbows reign supreme and love wins!" Lucas yells over the noise as he and Jamal step back.

Caleb waits until the noise settles and moves up to the mic.

"My name is Caleb, and I am also a proud gay man. I live

in a city called Bainesville." A shout goes up from the Bainesville crowd and Caleb laughs. "I work there in a community-based program that provides support for LGBTQ+ folks. Many cities have such programs, and I just want to let everyone know that there is always someone there to help when the going gets rough. Don't hesitate to reach out. Our information is on the Facebook page for this event. We can help get you connected, no matter where you live, so please, give us a call or drop us a line. Always remember, you aren't alone. We're a community and we will always be there to support you. Rainbows reign!"

People clap, flags fly, and posters wave back and forth as Caleb moves out of the way so that Ryan can take his place. I'm startled to see him there. He hates speaking in public even more than I do, and last time we talked about this, he said he wasn't going to do it. I wonder what, or who, changed his mind?

"Hi! I'm Ryan Malloy. I am not a gay man, but I am a proud man with cerebral palsy and I hate giving speeches, but Jack is making me do this."

Me? I didn't make him do it! Everyone laughs, and his friends from rehab start cheering. Clare is standing behind his chair with her hands lightly on his shoulders. She looks over at me and smiles sweetly. *Oh. Mystery solved.*

Ryan waits a minute and then tries to talk again.

"I have spent most of my life being the only guy in my school, or in my whole town, who has to use a wheelchair to get around. It's always been a challenge dealing with stairs, both the kind you have to get up and the kind that people shoot at you with their eyes. It's never easy being the only one, and when you are alone, you have to find something to help you figure out who you are. My family has always been really supportive, so I'm lucky there. And I found the swim team, which gave me something that's mine. But it's always been hard to live in a place where no one really understands what it means to be me, and that is why it means a lot to have the gang here today from my days in post-surgery rehab."

They all start hooting and hollering again, shouting "Disability Pride." Ryan smiles, but his face is starting to get really red and is clashing with his orange hair. Clare leans over and whispers something to him, and I can see him answer her. She looks over at me and shakes her head slightly. I walk over and take the mic from him.

"Thanks, Ryan. And Caleb and Lucas. I guess it's my turn now. My name is Jackson Pedersen. I am a proud gay man." My heart is pounding so hard that I'm sure it can be picked up by the sound system, but the cheering and applause drowns it out. I wait a few seconds and start again. "I've lived in Thompson Mills most of my life, and I've been hiding myself so far back in the closet for so many years that I never thought I'd see the light. I've been afraid to be myself in a place where being different is something too many people make fun of or put you down for. Sometimes they even threaten to hurt you because somehow they see you as a threat." I close my eyes for a second and take a deep breath. "I've been so afraid of my life that I wanted to end it last year until someone came along and changed my plans." I look over at Ryan, and he gives me a small thumbs up.

Everyone is silent now, listening to me as if I have

something important to say. It's beyond surreal, standing here sharing my life with so many people that I feel like I'm back in one of my dream hallucinations from last night.

"I don't want Thompson Mills to be a place where people have to be afraid. I don't want it to be a place where someone is run off the road just because he *isn't* afraid to be himself. We have to believe that we're better than that. We have to remember that a rainbow is made up of all different colors that work together to make the most beautiful sight in the sky." I look down at Benjamin and he gives me a tiny salute. Then I glance over at Lucas. "A friend once told me that the way to deal with fear is to bury it down so deep that someday you won't be able to find it anymore. Today, with this Thompson Mills Pride Parade, I'm starting to dig that hole. It's time to stop hating. We need to be kind to each other. That's all. That's everything. Rainbows reign and kindness rules!" The applause starts again, building until it sounds like hundreds of horses running wild and free across sun-baked fields. Flags are waving madly, and I can hear people shouting a mixture of every slogan we've used today.

I look over at Mr. Malloy and nod. He smiles at me, and ten seconds later music starts to swell out of the speakers beside me.

"This is all for you Benjamin," I call out loudly. "But I'm *so* not doing the voice," I add, looking down at him as he laughs and I start singing a song that was originally recorded by a frog. I've been practicing it for weeks just in case I found the courage to sing it for him some day.

I guess some day is here.

I make it through the song with lots of help from the crowd, many of whom decide to sing it à la Kermit, which makes for an absurd, messed-up cacophony—the sweetest choir I've ever heard. Benjamin is smiling from ear-to-ear, singing his heart out. I'm fairly certain his Kermit impression is the loudest and by far the most off key. It's wonderful.

As the music fades and the clapping starts again, I walk down the steps to where he's standing, still propped up by his rainbow cane. Ignoring everyone around us, I step under his protective bubble and put my hands on his shoulders, leaning in and giving him the best kiss I can find from somewhere inside of my imagination. He wraps one arm around me, kissing me back as everything around us disappears, and there's no one in the world but me and Benjamin. I can only manage one thought.

This is so much better than practicing with my pillow!

I hold on for a second more. I can feel something digging into my chest and I remember that I still have a piece of Benjamin's stone rainbow in my pocket. A red stone.

Red for life. *My* life.

I step back, feeling a little breathless. It takes a second for me to realize that we aren't really alone and everyone around us just saw me kiss a boy.

And it takes one more second for me to realize that it doesn't matter. I have nothing to hide. Not anymore.

I don't know what tomorrow is going to be like, and whether or not it will be all that different from yesterday around here. Today has been amazing, but I think it will be a while before anyone is going to be painting the old bridge in rainbow colors.

That's okay. I can wait. Because there is one thing I do know.

I'm not staying out of sight anymore.

I'm just staying out.

acknowledgments

I want to once again thank Margie Wolfe and all of the wonderful staff at Second Story Press for embracing my story and characters.

To Kathryn Cole, your unwavering support and patience is greatly appreciated.

Thank you to Kathryn White, editor extraordinaire, who found everything I missed and helped me give my characters some much needed balance. And I really enjoyed the fact that you took the time to comment on all of the words and phrases that you liked in the novel as well as those you felt needed some work. Everyone likes to read the compliments along with the constructive criticism!

To Jeffrey Canton who describes himself as a "storyteller, spoken word artist, bookseller, educator, writer, reader, and children's literature fiend," your insights on the manuscript were invaluable, particularly those regarding proper representation of the LGBTQ+ community.

Thanks to the Ontario Arts Council for continuing to support authors through funding initiatives such as the Writers' Reserve Grant.

And finally, to all of the young people (some of whom are not so very young anymore!) who have shared their lives and stories with me over the years. I admire your strength and courage in navigating a world that still provides more challenges than it should. I pray that someday each and every one of you can feel safe and accepted by everyone you meet as you travel your individual pathways.

Read more of Jack's story in Liane Shaw's previous book *Caterpillars Can't Swim*

"*Shaw has written a compassionate, well-crafted story about two boys dealing bravely with challenges and finding support in friendship.*"

—BOOKLIST

Included on IBBY's **Outstanding Books for Young People with Disabilities List** and **The Rainbow Book List** from the American Library Association.

When Ryan saves Jack from drowning, he is hailed as a hero in their small town. Ryan saves Jack's life, but he also keeps his secret. Their bond leads to a grudging friendship, and an unexpected road-trip to Comic Con, where they will both have the chance to push back against the stereotypes the world wants to define them by.

Ages 12+, $13.95
ISBN: **978-1-77260-053-7**

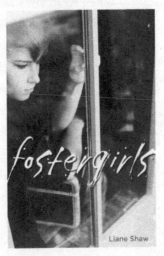